THE LOST ORCHARD

'There is a lot going on in this story: Paul's self-discovery; a respect for nature, and more than a hint of danger, which altogether makes for an impressive read'
Books Ireland

'What a debut! All the ingredients of the proverbial classic are in this novel … [it] brilliantly underpins the conflict between vested interests and selflessness, between ecology and industry. The characters bristle with authenticity … This gem of a book clamoured to be written and … is executed with pace and with passion and not a little humour'
InTouch

'A most moving book, with numerous positive messages slightly told, and with a tangible appreciation of the natural world'
The School Librarian

PATRICK DEELEY was born in Loughrea, Galway. He teaches in a primary school in Ballyfermot, Dublin. His poems have appeared in numerous magazines in Ireland and abroad, and he has published four collections with Dedalus Press. *The Lost Orchard* is his first story for children.

The LOST ORCHARD

PATRICK DEELEY

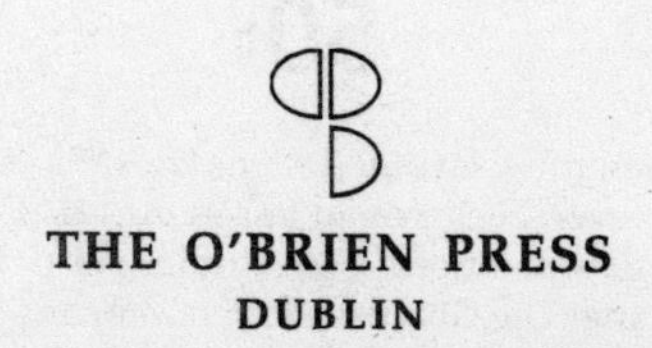

THE O'BRIEN PRESS
DUBLIN

First published 2000 by The O'Brien Press Ltd,
20 Victoria Road, Dublin 6, Ireland.
Tel: +353 1 4923333; Fax: +353 1 4922777
E-mail: books@obrien.ie
Website: www.obrien.ie
Reprinted 2001.

ISBN:0-86278-651-7

British Library Cataloguing-in-Publication Data
Deeley, Patrick, 1953–
The lost orchard
1.Children's stories
I.Title
823.9'14[J]

2 3 4 5 6 7 8 9 10
01 02 03 04 05 06 07

The O'Brien Press receives
assistance from

Editing, typesetting, layout, design: The O'Brien Press Ltd
Front cover, background image: Angela Clarke
Colour separations: C&A Print Services Ltd
Printing: The Guernsey Press Company Ltd

Contents

ACKNOWLEDGEMENTS

My thanks to Alan for the map; to Genevieve who read the early drafts; to Vincent and Simon for information about mining; to Marian Broderick, Íde ní Laoghaire, Michael O'Brien and all at The O'Brien Press for their encouragement and advice.

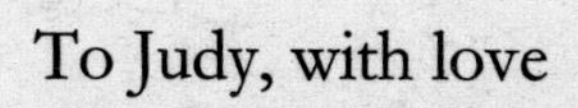

To Judy, with love

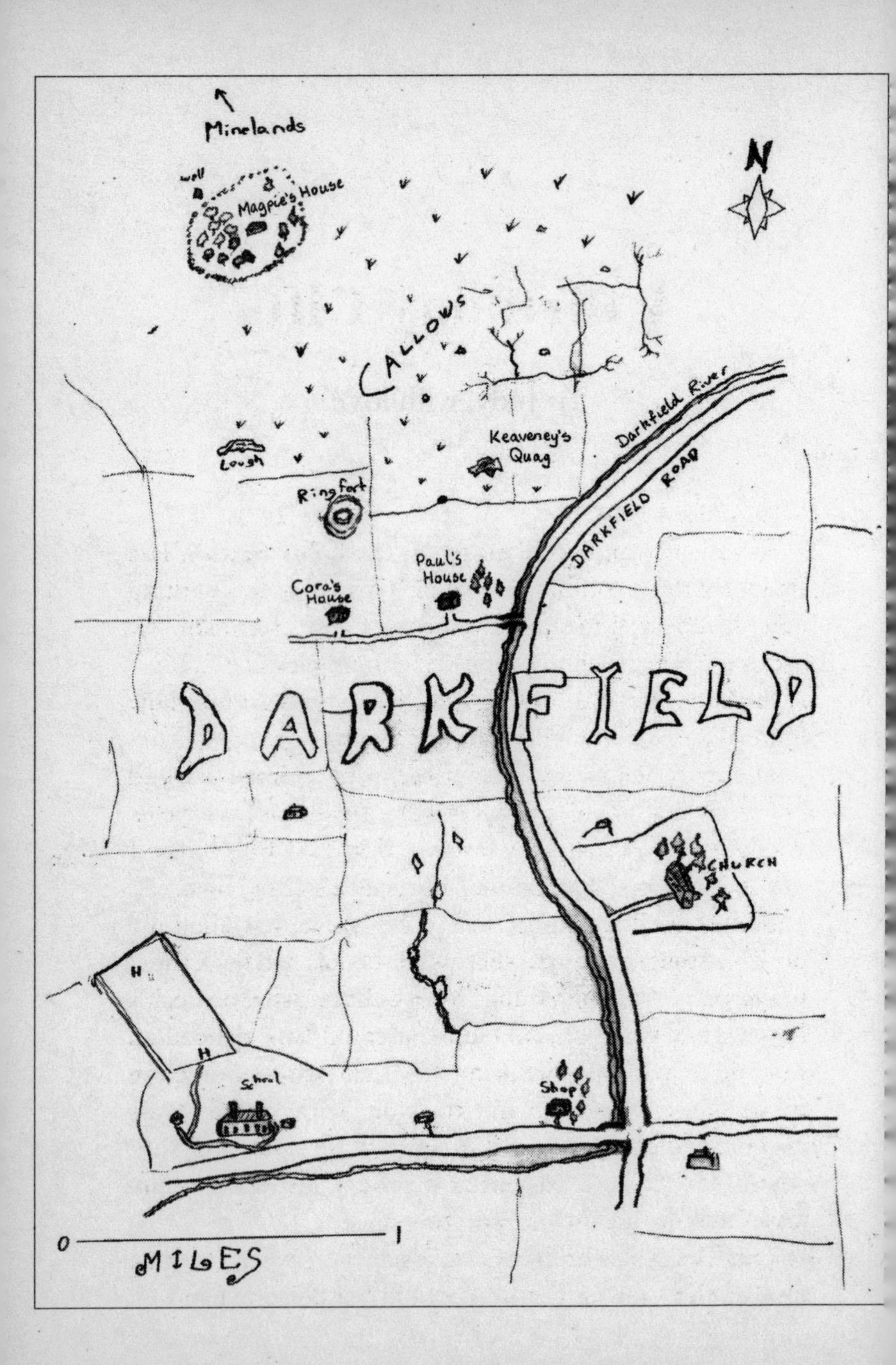

Minelands
N
well
Magpie's House
CALLOWS
Darkfield River
Keaveney's Quag
Lough
DARKFIELD ROAD
Ringfort
Paul's House
Cora's House
DARKFIELD
CHURCH
H
H
School
Shop
0
1
MILES

1

A Birthday Gift

'AT...ATT...ATTACK?'

Raymie Boland was struggling with his Sixth Class Reader at the top of the classroom. This scene was nothing new. It repeated itself, more or less, every afternoon. Mr McGrane, our teacher, trembled with impatience.

'Nooooo, Boland,' he sighed. 'Everybody knows how fond you are of attacking, but...try again.'

I kept my head down. Sometimes Mr McGrane dragged me in as a kind of prompter, though I was two years younger than Raymie, who was thirteen. But today I needed to keep a low profile – for reasons of my own.

So instead of catching the teacher's eye, I studied my desk – a stout oak model such as all schools had back then, in the year 1965 when things were built to last. The desk's legs were of cast-iron. An elephant could have danced on that desk without breaking it! Two white porcelain inkwells were set into the desktop, with sliding brass covers on them. We loved to snap these open and shut when Mr McGrane was out of the room, just for the pure joy of making a loud and irritating noise.

Cora Delaney, who always sat beside me, gave me a gentle kick on the shin, and smiled behind her delicate hand.

'Raymie's such a thicko,' she whispered.

I didn't smile back. A smile could be dangerous, under the circumstances. One of Raymie's pals might spot me. When the humiliating reading hold-ups started in Mr McGrane's class, the pals always glanced back at me. Salivating in anticipation of trouble. Because, often as not, I would have to go and read the word out for Raymie. And on such days, there would be a kickback. Raymie would make me pay later.

Right now, the word might as well be a big log thrown across Raymie's path – against which he kept miserably butting his head, to no avail.

'Att…e…att…'

Mr McGrane sighed. 'Come up, Pauly.'

The dreaded, familiar command always made me jump, no matter how often I heard it. And I had actually escaped hearing it for quite some time. By hiding, mostly. 'Come up and tell him, Pauly.'

Out of Mr McGrane's sarcastic mouth – the call to arms – filling the entire classroom. An order I dared not ignore. And yet...

I hesitated. Today, of all days, knowing the right answer didn't suit me. I could lose more than blood if I wasn't careful. Mam had made a deal with me. If I avoided trouble, she'd buy me an extra-special birthday present – *Captain Valour*, the American superhero comic. Issue 100: 'The Fires of Dr Sulphur'. Full colour. Extravagant artwork. Amazing plot-line. I simply had to have it. And there was only one day to go. Tomorrow would be my eleventh birthday.

I extricated myself from my desk and walked slowly to the top of the room. Raymie Boland stared at me, his long upper teeth pressing on his lower lip. His face was crimson red, and swarmed with golden freckles.

I felt almost sorry for him. Why couldn't he know the word? I had learned all my words from reading Captain Valour. I looked at Raymie's Reader, his black-nailed forefinger still glued to the spot.

I was about to pretend I didn't know the word – but then Raymie's eyes seemed to narrow, his lips formed a belligerent pout, and his head gave the smallest of shakes. And I understood his language. Raymie Boland, Sixth-Class muscleman, was giving me, plain Fifth-Class Paul Duggan, a health warning.

What would Captain Valour do? He'd live up to his name – that's what!

'Attempt!' I said brazenly at Raymie. 'The word is attempt!'

Something in his throat hastily swallowed this. His nostrils flared.

'Good man, Pauly,' Mr McGrane said. I had plucked him back from the brink of despair, one more time. 'You're right, as ever. Sit down.'

All heads turned with me as I walked back. Some wore pitying looks. They knew exactly what would happen. Another whacking for Pauly Duggan!

'Don't worry,' Cora whispered, removing her glasses and smoothing a stray lock of dark brown hair behind her ear. 'I can walk home with you today. They surely won't attack you while I'm there.' She smiled wickedly. 'They'd be afraid my mother would put the Evil Eye on them!'

This I found hard to believe. What thug would be warned off by a girl even younger and smaller than me, mother or no mother? Not Raymie, for sure.

But during the long, nervous wait to bell-time and home, with the serpents squirming and knotting in the pit of my stomach, I realised my only hope was Cora. Her mother, Mrs Delaney, went under the unofficial local title of 'Wise Woman of Darkfield' – a kind of white witch, if you like. She had an encyclopaedic knowledge of herbal remedies, and many people, including Raymie's mother, depended on her for relief from their various illnesses and allergies. It was rumoured that she could put the Evil Eye on you if you vexed her.

And as for Cora, she behaved so sensibly for a girl of 'ten--and-a-pick' that I sometimes felt I was dealing with someone a lot older.

The bell rang. Desks banged as everyone raced for the exit in a frenzy. Cora and I sprinted out of Darkfield School together, looking neither up nor down, hoping to beat the crowd and – in my case – make it home in one piece.

But Raymie and his pals were ahead of the posse. There they stood on the road home, blocking our way. They must have cut across the schoolyard and jumped over the fence to get to the road so quickly.

They started by shouldering me from right to left as I tried to pass. Then Raymie and his pal Hynes tried to give me a dig from the right – but they didn't dare hit Cora, who was standing between them and me.

'Pauly, Pauly, hidin' behind a woman's skirts,' Raymie scoffed, as the other kids laughed. Then he began mocking Mr McGrane. '"Come up, Pauly. Tell them, Pauly". Yeah, you can tell us all right! Tell us what it's like fer to be a coward!'

'You're yellow!' Hynes blazed close to my ear, and then Raymie spat out, 'Look at the yella streak all down yer back.'

'I suppose your mother will be over later to my mother, the Wise Woman, will she, Raymie?' Cora sneered, leaning across and prodding Raymie in the chest. 'What'll it be this time? Something for her back, or her legs – or her sorry excuse for a husband and son!'

'I...I wouldn't know anythin' 'bout them things,' Raymie faltered, backing off. 'Anyhow, thass women's business. And me da would pound ya if'n he heard ya sayin' them things.'

'Send him down to me, and I'll sort him out,' I blustered. 'And your uncles, while you're at it.'

I felt I ought to make some kind of show – for Cora's sake, you understand – but we didn't push it; we got out of there as fast as we could.

Just when we thought we were in the clear, a hail of clods from the ploughed field beyond Darkfield River landed around our ears. The fresh golden balls of clay shattered on our backs and the ones that didn't hit us spilled along the roadsides. Oh the indignity of it! My pride was cut to the quick. It was unheard of for Paul Duggan to run from a fight! And not only that, but in the shelter of a young girl and the protection of her mother!

Hopefully it would be worth it – keeping my promise to Mam, getting my hands on the Captain Valour magazine, Issue 100. Sacrifices, sacrifices. The Captain would understand.

'Just as well I was there to stand up to Boland,' I told Cora, after we had got away. 'But I do remember giving my word to your mother once that I'd always look after you.'

'Aah! Haa!' she sing-songed. 'That's the best joke yet!'

'No, it's true,' I replied. 'It's not just that we're neighbours. You're younger. And female. That's why your mother relies on me.'

'*You* rely on *me*!' Cora shouted. 'Didn't I just save your skin back there?'

'That's against the natural order, and was an exception,' I told her.

I flexed my biceps. 'This is the stuff that matters.'

Cora looked totally unimpressed. 'It's more than brawn that's needed in these situations,' she said, sharply. 'It was my brain got us out of that scrape.'

'Think that if it makes you feel better,' I mumbled.

Cora looked regretful, then. 'I should never have mentioned his mam and her visits,' she said, with a frown on her face. 'Or his da. It was wrong of me to…'

'I noticed the way he backed off when you said it,' I interrupted. 'Why did he do that?'

'His mother comes to my mother to get treatment for all her aches and pains. But really what's wrong with her is she's depressed. My mother gives her something called St John's Wort for it – it's a herbal medicine. I mean, wouldn't anyone be depressed, married to a man like Raymie's da? My mother says he spends all the money on drink and horses.'

"Well, anyway," I said, struggling to catch hold of another idea, 'Just say I had used my brain the way you did, it still wouldn't have worked. Raymie would have thumped hell out of me regardless. And that's because you're a girl, and I'm a fella.'

'No,' said Cora, patiently. 'It's because of the words I spoke. The words had power! They let Raymie and Hynes and the rest of that crew know they should be afraid of my mother, and what she might do to them!'

She seemed convinced she was right, but I wasn't likely to admit the power of mere words over brawn. Besides, Cora Delaney always insisted on having her own way. She'd wear you out with talk. And I told her as much. We were near my gate at this stage, and she pushed on ahead, not wanting to hear any more.

'Ungrateful,' she shouted back, but, of course, I didn't see it in those terms. I was simply thinking: 'One more day to go. Then Captain Valour will be flourishing his cape at 'The Fires of Dr Sulphur', with me ringside to watch it all.'

'Ah, here he is, the apple of my eye,' Mam said as I sauntered in the door of our farmhouse. 'And look! Not a bruise or a scratch on him anywhere.'

Mam always called me the apple. I thought it was getting a bit stale, to be honest, now that I was on the eve of my eleventh birthday. But I was Mam's only child, after all.

Mam and Dad had probably abandoned the idea of having children, since they were quite old – nearly forty years, maybe – when I arrived. Then, when I did come along, they made an extra fuss. Leastways, so I am reliably informed, since I can't remember the early part of it for myself.

And they weren't the only ones to rejoice. Because I happened to be the only child for several houses around – Cora Delaney didn't arrive until a year or so later, stealing some of my thunder – I was a wonder to my neighbours as well. Mrs Delaney, herself even older than Mam, said: 'That babe is a gift of nature delayed. It just goes to show, Mrs Duggan, nature will have its own way!'

For almost a year, until Cora came into the world, Mrs Delaney seemed as proud of me as if I were her very own.

'The blasted end of quietness', old John Hobbins proclaimed, whenever he heard me wailing. He actually meant this in a good way. He would hear my frequent shouts and squeals as he feebly walked about his farm, and they seemed to reassure him that he was still in the land of the living.

'There's hope for the village of Darkfield yet,' he announced, probably dreaming that he was at some long-lost hurling match or other, for he was well into his dotage, his second childhood.

Mam often reminisced about the event of my birth and how everyone had celebrated. Everyone called to our house for a 'look-see'. Far-flung relations came to visit where they'd never much bothered before. Even fussy Aunt Florence managed to tear herself away from what Mam always referred to as 'her imaginary aches and pains', in order to attend. For a time, I was, to enlarge on Mam's idea, the apple of every eye around.

One visitor, she told me, was particularly unexpected. An old, old man, with white and black streaked hair, who arrived from the far side of the village, riding a sturdy, jet-black pony. That man was called Magpie O'Brien, and he was proud and ancient and very strange. He climbed stiffly off the pony's back, outside our house, and handed the reins to Dad.

'He'll make a fine companion for the child, one of these days,' he said. 'Just give both of 'em time.'

'Come in, won't you?' Dad said. He and Magpie were friends.

'Is the priest within?' Magpie asked.

When Dad said yes, Magpie turned and wouldn't come in and walked homeward. He was a pagan, pure and simple. The last thing needed on my birthday was a debate – no, an argument – about God.

Of course I wasn't much aware of the pony Magpie gave me, at first. Dad began to introduce me to our various farm animals, after I had learned to walk. I met hens, ducks and geese for starters. One day, while I was taking in hen eggs from the big hay barn for Mam, the gander knocked me down and tried to pluck my hair out!

As I grew hardier, I was introduced to the bigger farm animals, pigs and sheep, and even the sad-eyed cows. Dad would let me sit on the sow's back while she rooted for earthworms in the haggard. She was a bit ticklish, but otherwise she didn't seem to mind.

When I was three, Dad told me, 'There's some fellow outside, and he's looking for a name.'

The pony waited solemnly at the big gate that led to the wide wild wet fields of what was known as our 'Callows'. Although, right then, I didn't look at the Callows – I had eyes only for the beautiful black animal.

'Hello, Jack!' I shouted. You'd swear I had known him by that name for all of my three earthly years.

'"Jack" it is, then,' Dad said with a smile.

I put my hand through the iron railing of the gate, and Jack nodded his long head down at me as if conceding that yes, the name was agreeable enough.

My own name was Paul – but nearly everyone insisted on adding a 'y' at the end of it. How I grew to hate that y! Aunt Florence had started calling me 'Pauly' on the very day I was christened, and before long the whole village had caught hold of it. Pauly this, and Pauly that! I couldn't do a hen's race, which is very little indeed, without some neighbour calling me Pauly.

Of course, at first, it didn't matter. Babies like baby names. They make them feel cared for and loved, and besides, what can babies do but put up with the names they've been given? It didn't matter much even when I was six or seven. But by the time I was eight I had educated my parents as to how they should address me. I would be

Paul to them. Nothing less, and certainly nothing more!

But Darkfield, my native village, was a different matter. It was full of ignoramuses, who didn't know how to address a man!

❦ ❦ ❦

'Mam,' I said, as we ate dinner. 'Aren't you going into town tomorrow to get a new perm?'

'And if you're not careful, that's all I'll get!' she chuckled, knowing I was hinting at the comic magazine, my birthday present.

Mam often gave us paper napkins at table. Dad always ignored his, and I usually found a use for mine other than the one intended. Today, I bored two holes in it for eyes, and made a slit for the mouth. I held it up to my face. Captain Valour's wine-red mask, what else? I said as much, in a big exaggerated American accent, then tried to flourish my end of the tablecloth about.

'Oops!' I said, as my half-cup of milk spilled.

'What class of language is "Oops"?' Dad scolded me, before turning towards Mam. 'Your son's head is full of nonsense,' he complained. 'Them comics have him ruined.'

'They're educational,' she said. 'Full of big words. That's why he can read so well, you know.'

I dabbled at the spilled milk with Captain Valour's scrunched-up mask.

'Did Mr McGrane ask you the books today?' Dad enquired.

'He did.'

'And?'

'And...I read fluently as a fish swims!'

'You're gifted,' Dad said, changing his opinion a full one hundred and eighty degrees from the one he'd held a few moments previously. I didn't tell about the downside to being gifted, though. The names, the threats, the clod-throwing...

'Paul has worked a big conversion, for a lad with pepper's own temper,' Dad continued.

'No more torn shirts, broken buttons, black eyes, bruised knuckles. Either he's winning all the fights with ease, or he's not fighting at all.'

He winked at me as he said the last bit. He was a big boxing fan.

He obviously didn't know about the deal I had made with Mam, concerning the fighting and a certain Captain Valour comic.

'I'm a little worried about what might happen tomorrow, Mam,' I said, and meant it. 'The name-calling's very bad.'

'Not that 'Pauly' business still, is it?' Dad interjected.

'Afraid so,' I said. 'Why do they keep calling me Pauly, Dad, when they know I hate it?'

He leaned back from the table, and grew expansive. He loved to 'explain' things to his supposedly 'gifted' son.

'This y letter's stubborn!' he said. 'It slips off people's tongues, and you can correct all you want, and hope they'll know better in future. Or you can pretend it doesn't matter a whole pile, can't you? Because it doesn't, surely. Didn't even your mother and I call you Pauly up until a few years ago?'

'But it's worse than just being called Pauly – those lads make me so angry,' I said bitterly.

'No silly name-calling is worth getting a nose-bleed over,' Mam said briskly. 'Just ignore them bullies. When they get no reaction, they'll quit.'

'They're better at making up insults than I am at playing deaf,' I told her. 'Especially the older fellows.'

I was hoping to gain some kind of insurance by talking it all out, so that she'd give me the comic regardless, but she just ruffled my hair. I'd have to play cautiously, next day. A good hiding would be nothing new, but the prize wasn't one that would come around again.

Mam wasn't the sort who would relent and give in if you didn't keep your part of the deal. No tears or cuts or bruises would sway her heart. Just the opposite, probably. They'd be a sign to say I hadn't changed, that I was still into trouble and mischief.

Next morning I sat with Cora as usual, but she kept to her edge of the desk. She was still annoyed after our argument, and we hardly spoke at all throughout the day. Close to lunchtime, I affected an illness, to avoid Raymie and the gang. But Cora tried to spoil my affectation by pretending *she* was ill as well! I reddened with anger at her – and this actually helped fool Mr McGrane. He placed the back of his hand against my forehead.

'A headache, boy,' he diagnosed.

'Yes sir,' I mumbled. 'I was up late last night. The sow was farrowing and I had to mind her by the infra-red light.'

'Farrowing' wasn't a word from my comic magazine, but 'infra-red' certainly was! At any rate, Mr McGrane seemed highly impressed.

'No wonder you've a headache,' he exclaimed. 'Such fine language would give a headache to anyone! You'd best stay in, I suppose.'

After break, I asked Cora if we might both walk home together.

'No,' she said flatly.

And that was that. If I wanted to avoid trouble, I'd have

to dream up something else.

At least Mr McGrane didn't ask me to read, figuring that I was still unwell. I probably looked unwell, too, what with worrying about Raymie and his gang. They felt they owed me a hiding. I saw them whispering up the front seats, then turning their heads to grin back at me. Once, when Mr McGrane wasn't looking, Raymie turned and eyed me, and put his trigger finger to the side of his head. I read the movement of his silent lips. 'Bang!'

It didn't look healthy, that's for sure. I could plead with Cora, but no, pride wouldn't let me, and pride can be the ruination of a person. Besides, she looked so virtuous now, methodically going about her lessons – let Cora scratch!

The home bell rang and, as Mr McGrane abdicated his rule for another day, everybody bundled simultaneously out the door, or tried to at least. I hung back. Then I sneaked – not through the school gate to the left – but right, into the lone-standing grey lavatory. I bolted the door behind me, then stood on the wooden toilet seat, and gaped out the ventilation space above the door.

All the children were well away, heads bobbing into the sunlit distance, bags on backs, carefree. Then I caught sight of Raymie and his three henchmen – delaying, moping about. They seemed confused, wondering where I was. They glanced back once. Then they took off at a fast pace, thinking no doubt to overtake me up ahead.

I could have cheered. It was a move worthy of Captain Valour himself, and Issue 100 was as good as in my clutches. I imagined the two of us – Valour and me – battling each other. Super heroes sometimes did that. Due to a misunderstanding, usually. It always ended in a draw, so that neither hero lost face. Not losing face was vital. Yeah, let Cora scratch! Let Raymie stew in his own angry juices!

I heard the teachers' cars pull away. I waited another few minutes, then I unbolted the lavatory door and slipped homeward.

It was a beautiful evening – the evening of my birthday! My house was about three miles from Darkfield School, but I resisted the urge to hurry. There was a gentle breeze at my back. Darkfield River flowed merrily alongside the road for most of my journey. I grew calm and dignified. I strolled. The river gurgled. I met no traffic. Soon we would go barefoot, with the warm weather.

I popped into Tommy Hodgkins' shop at Darkfield Cross. Tommy lifted from studying the death notices in the newspaper. He was fond of reading the death notices. His ginger eyebrows twitched. He seemed in an unusually good humour today. Maybe his worst enemy has died, I thought to myself.

'Ah, if it isn't the Duggan dynamo!' he exclaimed.

My penny bought twenty bull's-eye sweets. Twice the usual amount.

'Tommy, you must know it's my birthday,' I said, and he shovelled in a few extra clove sweets from another can.

At Darkfield Cross, the river turned with me and passed under a bridge. The hawthorn bushes to either side showed countless white blossoms. These gave off a scent that made me sneeze. I stuck a bull's-eye in my mouth. It burned my tongue and throat pleasantly.

The breeze rustled the hawthorns ahead. Was it the breeze? Or was there something else? The bushes rustled some more.

'Relax,' I told myself.

I heard the sharp crack of a branch, and I stopped dead in my tracks. Raymie Boland had jumped out onto the road.

'Howya, Pauly,' he said, with a toothy grin.

Next moment Pad Burns, one of his gang, joined him. Pad was gangly-limbed and pasty-faced. He lurched into the road rather than jumped.

'Sorry, Raymie,' he mumbled.

'We're goin' to teach ya a lesson, Pauly,' Raymie said, ignoring him. 'If'n ya like, you can call it payback time fer all the schoolin' help you give us.'

'Yeah,' pasty-faced Pad said. 'We're gonna teach you a lesson about spattered brains.'

I should run – now! Run as fast as I could, back the way I had come. Immediately the impulse died. I heard a rustling sound behind me and Dervan and Hynes, Raymie's two other henchmen, appeared. They didn't bother with any dramatics. You could almost say that they stole out, but the fright I got was no less intense for that.

'Goin' someplace?' Hynes casually quizzed.

'Goin' noplace,' Dervan answered.

They often played this kind of game, a version of good cop, bad cop, which we all knew from TV – only problem being that both were bad cops.

'Goin' to swot?' Hynes quizzed again.

'Goin' to swot the swot!' Dervan responded.

The four gang-members closed on me. I stood rooted to the spot. Raymie was nonchalant as he directed the others. His long upper teeth pressed into his lower lip, his face was as freckled as the large egg I had found once on the edge of the Callows – but not nearly as charming.

I felt none of the quick fieriness that a fight, or the prospect of a fight, usually brought. As I tightened my fingers into fists and lifted my leaden arms, I was reluctant. I hadn't a hope. There were *four* of them!

Hynes and Dervan pinioned me by my arms while Pad

and Raymie punched me in the face and stomach. I tasted my own blood, then a moment later the stinging pain sprang to my lip. There was a sudden brightness in my left eye, which immediately closed tight. A low blow plunged into the pit of my stomach. I felt sick and slumped onto the roadside, no longer much aware of anything at all.

When I came to, I was lying on my back among ferns and tall grasses. My ambushers had gone. My face was bleeding, and only the one eye would function. A dark pain throbbed in my head. I turned my head and spat out blood and splinters of bull's-eye. I fumbled in my pocket. Of course they had taken my bag of sweets.

I lay there for a long time. It seemed the most restful thing to do. It seemed almost to dam the pain I knew was welling through every part of me.

But slowly I sat up. I got to my feet. Flexed myself. No bones broken. Only pain. I could live with that. I spat more blood, and what seemed to be a fragment of tooth. Everything was deathly quiet.

Then, from somewhere in the distance, I could hear a droning sound, growing nearer. At first I assumed it was a car, but the sound grew louder and louder, until it was incredibly loud. It seemed to be closing in on me from overhead.

I tipped my head back and peered through the sunlight, forcing my good eye to focus, and saw the black arrow-shape of a plane directly above. It was flying so low that I felt suddenly afraid. It seemed to be searching – for what or for whom I didn't know. Its metal wings were spread wide as if they might somehow gather up the entire earth and make off with it.

I craned my neck to follow its flight-path and, completely overreaching myself, fell backwards. Captain

Valour bites the dust – twice in one episode! My head spun. By the time I got to my feet, the plane had gone, leaving only a faint grumble behind with me where I stood on the roadside.

❦ ❦ ❦

'Oh Paul, God help us, look at the state of you!' Mam shrieked when she saw me at the door.

'It wasn't me started it, Mam, honest!' I spluttered.

'Oh, child! Come on, let me clean you up,' she said, putting her arm about my shoulder.

Dettol, cotton swabs, bandages, the lot. I didn't even bother to ask about the Captain. He was far away, well out of bounds. I headed numbly for the stairs.

'Paul!' Mam said.

I looked around.

'Happy birthday, child.'

There, in her open hands, despite everything, was Issue 100! And Captain Valour himself on the cover, enchained by flames. He seemed in nearly as much trouble as I was. I smiled, though it made my lips hurt. Clutching the super hero to my chest, I climbed to my room.

The glossy covers felt so smooth that they almost slipped through my fingers. The inside pages were packed with all-colour action. Exquisite, astounding scenarios flowed through pages dipped in gold dust. Each panel spewed words, words, elaborate new-fangled words – and exclamation marks were sprinkled everywhere. America, what a place! New York, what a crazy metropolis! Strange though it may seem, as I lay in my early bed, 'The Fires of Dr Sulphur' soothed my aching heart.

2

Across the Callows

MY INJURED EYE CHANGED from black to purple to yellow, and my face finally cleared to its usual freckled white. My cut lips grew scabs. I plucked these carefully as they ripened. I got up and walked. The sobs left my chest. I breathed freely again. It all took only a matter of days. And, of course, it gave me some time off school.

Cora and her mother called. The Wise Woman had heard the news already from Mam, and she brought some peculiar herbal remedy for my wounds. Arnica, I think she called it – extracted from yellowish dried flower heads.

'Just a tincture, Mrs Duggan,' she explained. 'Apply it to the bruises.'

Her cure seemed a bit feeble to do much good, but I said thanks anyway. If Mrs Delaney was a witch, white or otherwise, she didn't look like one. Except maybe for her long straight silver hair, flowing down her back. I'd have said grey, but Cora said no, silver was appropriate when a woman reached a certain age. Mrs D was frail enough, though, frailer than you'd expect a witch to be. She even had a lame step, and she wore thin-rimmed glasses. No evidence of the evil eye Cora had told me about.

After the medical ministrations from the Wise Woman,

Cora and I went into the back room. Now Cora began to wring her hands a bit.

'I feel awful, Paul,' she said, eventually. 'About what happened. I could have stopped it happening. Probably I could.'

'How?'

'If I'd walked home with you when you asked,' she said, remorsefully.

'I never asked. Leastways, I don't remember asking.'

She looked at me as if she were about to scream, but instead she took off her glasses, pushed her hair back from her face, and put her glasses on again. A calming gesture, that's how I read it.

'Why do you get into so many fights, Paul?' she said next. 'I know about Boland's gang. I know all that stuff about them resenting you when Mr McGrane asks you to read for them. But he asks other boys to do the same, and they don't get beaten up for it. Why you?'

'I'm an outsider,' I said, liking the sound of that. It made me feel like Captain Valour – another outsider. But she wasn't half so impressed.

'You lose the rag over nothing,' she said. 'Even being called 'Pauly' is enough to wind you up.'

'Maybe once,' I asserted. 'Not any more. It takes more than that to upset me now. It's just that I'm different from them somehow! And they know it. That's why Boland has a set against me.'

Cora wouldn't be pacified. Everyone's different, she reminded me. And that I wasn't half as smart as I imagined. If I was smart, I wouldn't let thickos like Raymie goad me into fights I could never win.

So much for sympathy, Cora Delaney-style!

❦ ❦ ❦

Dad, however, said I had the gift of quick healing – like him. He was secretly proud of me, I think, for trying to stick up for myself, as he saw it. If he'd seen the poor battle I'd put up, he might not have been so impressed.

'I'm sure them other lads are in a much worse condition than you, Paul,' he said. But maybe he was just trying to restore my pride.

'I saw a small aeroplane flying really low over the village as far as the Callows,' I told him. 'I think it was a single-engine one.'

'After you'd been knocked down, is it? That's your imagination.'

'After I'd stood up again,' I said. 'I definitely saw it.'

'Imagination,' he repeated, not really listening to me. 'Fighters often dream when they're knocked down.'

Then he gave me a big wink, and I was almost inclined to believe him. Dad was what you might call a persuasive blusterer.

But two days later, the plane returned. And this time it had brought a companion. Together they moved low over the village of Darkfield – back and forth in perfectly straight lines across the small flat fields. They did this again and again, always whirling around as soon as they reached the broad unfenced Callows.

Our cows looked up from their grazing, then carried on chewing the cud. I saw Jack, the pony, surge to the wet fastness of the Callows, where he seemed slowly to sink, a distant black speck. Mam's geese flew, and abruptly landed again. The sow started a strange grunting, her head tilted up sideways as if she were questioning the sky. And our flock of sheep took off in a flurry to the far corner of the lower field, where they huddled almost in a heap. Maybe they saw the planes as huge droning black mechanical crows, swooping to devour their lambs.

'God, Paul, but you weren't wrong,' Dad admitted, watching the continual to-and-fro flight of the small aircraft.

But why had the planes come? This question bothered me as much as the next person. I conducted my own survey. Some of the answers I received showed that a strange breed of people lived in Darkfield. Apparently, we had big imaginations, and a complete lack of common sense.

'Them's spy planes sent by the Rooshians,' old John Hobbins said.

I discounted his theory. I figured the Russians would be much too busy trying to outrun the Americans to the moon. They'd already got a man in space before them, but now the Americans had caught up. Besides, what was there to spy on in Darkfield, apart from second-hand threshing machines and antiquated tractors?

'Don't you know well they're spraying the fields with a new chemical that might kill grass fluke and murrain and suchlike cattle diseases?' Mick Delaney – Cora's Dad – told me.

'Invisible spray?' I quizzed.

'Invisible is right, Pauly,' he said, 'and my Missus, the Wise Woman, disapproves of it.'

I didn't believe him either.

There were nearly as many theories as there were people. The commotion brought by the planes spread throughout the village. Everyone sounded feverish; everyone acted giddy. I decided at last to give Dad another chance.

'They're filming landscapes for an Irish Western,' he said, but then a smile broke over his face.

I gave up my survey as a dead loss. I couldn't tell who was being funny and who was being stupid. Me, I hadn't a clue, and besides, I was busy recovering my powers after the ambush.

The shadow of school crept closer and closer. Then finally, one morning, the inevitable happened. Mam said, 'You're fit again.' I dragged myself past Darkfield Cross and along by the gurgling river, feeling as Captain Valour must have done one time when he'd been bound in irons by the robot, Metallus Rex.

My wounds proved to be a one-minute wonder. I hung glumly about the yard, waiting for lessons to commence. Friends were thin on the ground. Why should this be, I wondered. Maybe Boland's gang had put the frighteners on everyone. Maybe, as Cora said, I was a big-head, always blundering on to my next, ever-deserved comeuppance.

'Soft day, eh?'

'Nah! Soft Pauly!'

Hynes' and Dervan's little hello. Then Pad Burns said: 'You'll have to stop runnin' into them blackthorns, Pauly. Bad for the complexion, like.'

A gaggle of youngsters laughed at that, but Cora immediately said: 'Hear who's talking about complexions, everyone? Pasty-face Pad!'

The laugh sounded louder now.

'Shut up, Four-eyes!' Pad shouted.

'Only intelligent people wear glasses, Pad Burns,' Cora replied. 'My mother, the Wise Woman, says so.'

'Oh yeah?' Pad said. 'That's how come she got to be a so-called Wise Woman, is it?'

He sounded uncomfortable, saying 'Wise Woman'. And

he might as well have waved a white flag, because everybody jeered at his poor response.

Raymie Boland arrived almost late, as was his habit. He came towards me slowly.

'If'n,' he said, screwing up his face as he inspected mine, 'If'n ya squeal, Pauly Duggan...'

But he didn't finish, because the rusty old bell rattled, and we all traipsed towards our lining-up spot.

'Good God, what happened to your face?' Mr McGrane asked, as soon as he clapped eyes on me.

'I'm not at liberty to say,' I replied carefully.

'Not at liberty, eh?' His tone hardened.

'No. Not really.'

'Not really! But we can hazard a guess, can't we, Pauly?' He shot a look at Raymie who was staring innocently out towards the hurling field.

The morning always began with drill. We raised our hands, then let them fall to our sides, as ordered by Mr McGrane. We stuck them out as if about to glide free of the concrete playground, and again let them fall. We finger-tipped the shoulders of the person in front, and once more let our hands fall. We repeated these actions several times, to Mr McGrane's barked commands. Then we trooped to our classroom.

After a while, someone mentioned the planes.

'Ah, the planes, the planes,' Mr McGrane said wearily. 'Everywhere I go, I hear the same refrain. Why are there planes flying over Darkfield? That's nearly as big a mystery as the marks on Pauly Duggan's face.'

The class laughed. Everyone except Raymie Boland, strangely enough. He just frowned a bit.

Mr McGrane was tall, sallow-skinned, white-haired. He always wore the same pin-stripe suit. There was chalk-dust on the cuff of his right sleeve, too indelible to wash out after long years writing at the blackboard. I felt no different from anyone else in Darkfield – and I don't just mean the school – I feared Mr McGrane big-time. He had a pulse plain to see on the left side of his face, beating like a tadpole's tail in a Callows pool. You could read Mr McGrane by that pulse. If it beat slowly, he was safe. You could almost joke with him. If it beat fast, best keep your head down and stay quiet. Today, the pulse was moderate to quick.

'I'll tell you, boys and girls, why the planes have come,' he continued, sounding bored. 'They come bearing cartographers.'

'Cart – what, sir?' Raymie Boland asked, taking his courage in his hands. He often showed a touch of gumption in class, but nobody thanked him for it, least of all Mr McGrane.

'Map-makers to you, Boland. They're making a map of Darkfield – the last place on Earth to be discovered.'

We could all recognise an insult when we heard it. This one didn't even have the grace to be clever. But still we smiled for Mr McGrane's benefit.

❦ ❦ ❦

Cora and I walked home together after school. We simply fell into step, that's all. There was no talk of anyone minding anyone, or of anyone owing anyone for being minded. I didn't see us as complete equals, of course. I was a year older and, officially at least, I was still the minder. But I let the subject sit.

'Not that I couldn't do it,' I said to Cora, 'but thanks for shooting down Pad Burns.'

She shrugged. 'It's mean to pick on one person,' she

said, 'and they were picking on you.'

'If you're not careful, they'll be picking on you, too,' I advised her.

'They won't,' she answered. 'See how Pad froze when I talked about the Wise Woman?'

'She must have great power, your Mam,' I said, purely for the devil of it.

'She has no more power than the man in the moon!' Cora exclaimed. 'It's just that they all think she has power.'

'No evil eye?'

She laughed. 'Evil eye, my foot! Did you really believe me when I told you that before, Paul?'

'No, I suppose not.'

'She *is* a healer, though. She learned it from her mother. She'll teach it to me some day.'

I knew the witchy stuff was untrue, yet I felt disappointed, hearing it confirmed for definite by Cora.

'I thought she was deeper than that, your mother,' I said.

'She is deep!' Cora insisted. 'She gives me the right power words to use, after all. Letting me talk about the Evil Eye, and calling her the Wise Woman all over the place. She knows it helps me out if anyone tries to bully me.'

'Oh right,' I said, beginning to see a bit more clearly what Cora was getting at, but disappointed still. 'I just wish...'

'What?'

'I just wish I had a power word or two of my own,' I told her.

❦ ❦ ❦

One person would surely know the truth about the planes – or so Dad assured me. That was Magpie O'Brien, the man who had brought the gift of the pony when I was born. I had never properly thanked Magpie, of course. How could I? By the time I understood about the gift, it was gone past the stage of saying thanks. I did mumble something once, but the idea of it was so odd that the words came out crooked and embarrassing.

It wasn't as if I knew Magpie well, or anything. He was a difficult man to locate. Never seemed to fit in with the rest of the farm-folk in Darkfield. Never went to church or pub or hurling match. Did his shopping in town. Bought his newspapers in a shop in the busy little village of Kilmere, some miles distant. Lived in a lonely, backward spot beyond the Callows, which placed him out of my reach, so to speak. For I was forbidden to cross the dangerous Callows. And no road could lead me to his house.

'If the planes are giving you so much worry,' Dad said, 'won't I find out from Magpie?'

'When? Tonight?'

'Ah no. It'll be a week, maybe two, at the earliest. I've enough to do, with the oats to be sowed, and whatnot. Anyway, he wouldn't expect me now.'

'But isn't his a visiting house? Couldn't you go over and talk, and play cards any night you like?'

'I could,' Dad agreed. 'But there'd be no atmosphere. Talk and cards need the dark winter nights in order to be effective. No. I'd only inconvenience Magpie if I went over now.'

Dad's answer frustrated me greatly.

'Is Magpie wiser than the Wise Woman?' I asked Mam.

'She's wiser,' Mam said.

'Is the Wise Woman wiser?' I asked Dad.

'Magpie's wiser,' Dad said.

I nearly caused a ruckus between my peace-loving parents, with such questions.

'He's the last of the independents,' Dad asserted. 'A pure pagan.'

Mam didn't like that kind of talk.

'It would be more in his line to go to church like any God-fearing Christian,' she said. 'A pure pagan indeed! Whatever next?'

'Haven't I seen him?' Dad said. 'He has powers, that lad, I tell you.'

'What powers?' I wanted to know.

'Well, for instant,' Dad said, becoming expansive again. (He meant to say 'for instance', but I stayed hush.) 'Weren't we playing poker one night when the rooster flew up from beside the fire, and scattered Magpie's hand. He had a winning hand, Magpie had, a straight flush of spades, and the cards fell everywhere. Didn't he curse that rooster down dead before our very eyes!'

'Nonsense,' Mam said. 'A man who keeps roosters inside his house, how could you credit him?'

'One rooster,' Dad said. 'And several hens. Didn't old John Hobbins see the same thing as me? Ask him if you please.'

'I will not!' Mam flared. 'I don't need to be told what is codology and what isn't. And you should know better than filling the child's head with nonsense.'

I quite liked the nonsense. I wouldn't mind hearing more of it. I had become intrigued by now, but also a little bit afraid of Magpie, to tell you the truth. Intrigued not just to see if he knew about the planes. For he had become painted in my mind as exotic, colourful, even dangerous. And what appealed to me equally was that he seemed a total outsider, which was just the thing I liked to imagine about myself.

Mam withdrew into her magazine. She always did that

after a row with Dad. 'Now look where your questions have led?' he said accusingly to me. He then made a cup of cocoa for Mam. She took it grudgingly.

'I only meant,' Dad said, 'that Magpie has great mental powers. He reads three newspapers every day, the only person I know who does that. He knows about far-off places. The Amazon, Siberia, the veldt of South Africa – Magpie talks about such places without let or hindrance. Sport, politics, commerce – he seems to understand the world even when the world is a confusion to itself.'

Dad relaxed. He had surprised me greatly with his speech, and now he had finished. But he wasn't given much time to float in his spatial glory, because there was no one better than Mam to knock a person back down to Earth when she felt they deserved it.

'If he's so wonderful,' she said, 'why don't you go over and live with him?'

An idea hit me then. It flew straight out of Mam's words, and into my brain. I decided to consult Cora before acting on it. Next evening I saw her cycling on the lane outside, and went to talk to her.

'Come across the Callows with me,' I suggested.

'The Callows? No, I couldn't. I'd be thrashed if I went. And you know what happened before, don't you? I nearly got drowned in Keaveney's Quag. And me barely on the edge of it!'

She shivered at the memory, then yanked her handlebars back firmly towards the middle of the road.

'That must be, oh, two or three years ago,' I reasoned. 'You've grown up a lot since then. And I know all the dangerous spots. We could easily avoid them.'

'No, Paul. I won't go. And you shouldn't go either.'

'I have to go,' I told her. 'Magpie O'Brien lives beyond

there, and I need to talk to him.'

'Him!' she exclaimed, pushing off. 'Why would you want to talk to him?'

'To ask about the planes.'

She half-turned her head, saying she would have nothing to do with my mad schemes.

'Don't tell my Mam,' I yelled after her, but she cycled off without answer.

I will admit Cora did have a bad experience with the Callows – it's no fun nearly being drowned. But what can you do? Wait for someone to grow up a bit more? Hardly! I was sorry I had confided in her. The Captain would never have confided. That was the essence of lonerdom. That was part of his – our – mystique.

I would visit Magpie alone, just to sound him out. Because now the planes had moved on from our part of Darkfield, to boom and grumble like distant thunder beyond the Callows – where his thatched cottage stood.

❦ ❦ ❦

I set off the following day after school. My parents would have forbidden the visit – on account of the Callows, but maybe, in Mam's case, on account of Magpie too – so I didn't tell my parents. Reckless or brave, or plain disobedient, that's the way it happened. 'Inconsiderate' might be the word I'm reaching for. But the Callows were something that had always stood in my path, and at the same time presented me with a dream – to cross over, to find out what lay on the far side.

Even the word 'Callows' was something no dictionary could explain to me. For no dictionary contained that word. And I didn't want to ask Mr McGrane.

'Callows, hmm?' Mam said, once, when I asked her. 'That must come from 'callow', with a small 'c'.'

'I found that word all right,' I told her. 'It means 'raw'.

'Well, won't 'raw' do you, child? Aren't the Callows raw land, don't you think?'

'I suppose so,' I said doubtfully.

Now I resolved to ask Magpie about the Callows, as well as the planes.

I crossed my last stretch of home ground before reaching the Callows. There was a large boundary stone at this point, one my hands knew well. I turned it over carefully, just to check on the creature that lived underneath. Yes, there he was – long, coal-black, passing himself off to the world at large as a scrap of cinder. But boy could he move when I tickled him with my finger! And his tail curved back at me in an evil-looking gesture that yet was perfectly harmless. I'd come to regard him almost as a pet by now, and again I said his name.

'Devil's coach-horse.'

A superb name for an insect, surely, but time was pressing. I eased the heavy stone down over him, and stepped into the Callows.

The Callows were many landscapes. Hay meadows, bogs and marshes. They contained traps and ambushes that would put Raymie Boland and his gang to shame. The danger was gradual, though. No great fuss at first. The start of an outback, tiny compared to the Australian Outback Mr McGrane had shown us on a globe at school. Tiny and very different – but an outback to my mind at least. I walked the last good grazing, and glimpsed away to my left the ring-fort that belonged to Cora's Dad.

On and on I walked through thick mud, my wellingtons squelching, my heart a big frog, ready to leap into my mouth at any moment. I feared the Callows, and Dad said that in certain cases fear was healthy. He wouldn't have approved of me going without permission, that much I knew for certain.

'I'll show you, Dad,' I shouted to the breeze. 'I'll be the second-last of the independents!'

Of course, I was shouting simply to bolster myself, for the Callows grew more and more thin-skinned, and they began to shiver underfoot. My shouts didn't stop the dread thoughts from entering my head. What if the thin skin broke? Would I sink? Down, down, into a swallow-hole I might go. Until only my head showed, and then only the top of my head! And I pictured the thin, almost liquefied skin sealing itself deceptively over.

I had to make several stops, to 'do a courage-check', as Captain V often said. Again I stepped gingerly along. No part of the Callows was more treacherous than Keaveney's Quag. How Cora managed to be playing here I couldn't imagine. I'd ask her some time. But today Keaveney's Quag was obvious enough, from where I stood. And where I stood was a good stride back from it!

Long blades of grass and matted weeds grew over its edges, but the middle was clear as daylight. I pictured a dragon's liquid eye, reflecting back the clouds and the blue sky. The dragon himself was under the Earth. His long thin water-body ran a mile or so ahead of me, hidden in its lair, until a spring emerged – his tail. Dad said it was from this dragon's tail that Magpie drew his supply of water, cold and pure.

In between Keaveney's Quag and Magpie's well lay the Callows and their several swallow-holes – as sly as nature could make them. I sloshed through clusters of tall wild iris, which we called flaggards, and I looked around. The flaggards reached to my waist. Some had put out yellow flowers; others purple. And rushes proliferated everywhere. Moths and butterflies hugged these, craneflies also. But such wildflowers sprouted amid open patches of herb and grass as would thieve the sight from your eyes! I didn't know many of their names, nor did I look too long at them – I was busy concentrating on swallow-holes!

Here they waited for my false step. There they pretended to be decayed mats of just so many old brown rushes, minding their own business. When I avoided them in one place, they turned up in another, disguised differently. Some presented shallow pools slicked with rust-traces of iron, which I found attractive to look at. Others offered cosy cushions of moss, fit for a king's bottom.

I didn't sit, but instead moved on to a quick small stream criss-crossing the Callows. A second stream, then a third and a fourth, followed after that. I studied each before leaping over it. Some were simple gashes in the dark earth. Others had high mounds on their banks where they had been dragged and deepened. And hidden boulders. And funny little stone bridges. I watched my step. You could break an ankle, no bother. Then who would come to get you? Nobody, probably. For the Callows were lonely, with no houses near.

Yes, the Callows were wild, and dangerous – even now, though winter had passed, and there'd been no rain for a while. But I felt full of wonder as I walked.

Once I nearly stepped on a hare nesting in his little form made of rushes. Then I found my foot poised above a quagmire. 'Madness,' I said to myself, drawing back. Soon a gentler surprise – a vixen leaping in broad daylight, trying to catch a moth. Seeing me, she moved slowly off. I couldn't help thinking that she resembled a shroud, a reddish shroud on legs!

Somewhere near, the curlew made a wounded, whistling sound. I remembered Dad's words. 'When the curlew whistles, it's a sign of rain.' Next moment, I heard the snipe. Its low bleating was created, Dad had assured me, by the wind through its tail-feathers.

And I looked at the black mud clinging to my wellingtons, and tried to shake it off. But the mud moved, extended itself. Then I saw it was a leech. Its strange, tapered head and tail fascinated me, its body-segments looped a step higher along my boot, sensing warmth, sensing flesh to fasten onto... I found a shank of weed and brushed it away, back to its dark clayey bed.

I looked up. I was through the Callows! I did a congratulatory jig, splashing my clothes in the process. And there in the distance I saw Magpie's chimney, smoking calmly. 'His little house is in good need of a fresh thatch,' I told myself.

(So was his head, last time I'd seen it, which had distinctive streaks of black and white hair. Was that why they called him Magpie, I wondered. Or maybe it was his jaunty way of walking? It might be impolite to ask. Nicknames were delicate subjects, as I knew only too well.)

The most remarkable thing about Magpie's set-up was the fine orchard beside it, of freshly leafed apple trees. I counted ten trees in all, shut behind a privet hedge. This hedge ran in a wide sweep from the cast-iron gate of his haggard to another gate at the haggard's far end. Some few of the branches leaned over the gate. Others ascended the nearby shed, which faced in towards the haggard and whose roof was of pale red galvanise. I stretched my hands upward, able to touch the apple trees. And every branch blossomed white.

I climbed the chained gate with difficulty. It shook as I

balanced on top. Then, leaning my weight on one arm, I swung over and down with a thump. Magpie's sheepdog, Riff-raff, came towards me with his head held low and his tail wagging in a big show of friendship.

I wasn't fooled for a second. I knew Riff-raff's game well from stories Dad had brought home. He would sneak around behind you, Riff-raff would, and nip at your softest flesh. Then away he'd move, casual as you please, still wagging his tail and without so much as a bark or a growl.

Yes, Riff-raff was wicked. And, I might add, very strange. But I didn't think about that now. Instead I timed the heel of my wellington to lift just as he closed in behind me, and caught him sharp under the chin! I took a risk, timing it like that, but there was nothing to hand, short of breaking a branch from one of Magpie's orchard trees.

Magpie had good hearing for an old fellow. Eighty years and a bit, people declared, though nobody could be certain. He came stiffly out of his white-washed house, pointing a warning.

'Mind that dog! Riff-raff, come 'ere this minute!'

Riff-raff ran to heel, quick.

'Ah, he's sedate enough,' Magpie said, patting him.

'He's very kind,' I pretended. 'Does he bark at all?'

'He don't. That's on account of the foxes,' Magpie said. 'He hears them vixens barking at night, sure he smells them on the wind, don't he. He knows they're there. And ain't that enough for him? What cause has he to be barking, on the edge of the wild, near his kinfolk?'

'He's not a fox, though,' I suggested. 'He's a sheepdog, surely?'

'He's half of one and four-eighth of the other,' Magpie said. 'Them's approximate figures, mind.'

True enough, Riff-raff did have the reddish coat and the

pointed features of a fox, but I thought Magpie was stretching it a bit, just the same. Something about that dog wasn't right, though. And, just for insurance, I kept a close eye on his movements throughout.

'Riff-raff's a great name for him,' I said, trying to be conversational. 'How did you come up with it?'

'Ah now,' Magpie said warmly. 'He done the rounds, that dog did. I believe every second farmer in the parish turned him down eventually. They said he was a dead loss. And when there was no alternative, he came to see what I'd make of 'im. The name occurred to me the minute we clapped eyes on each other. Riff-raff he was, and Riff-raff he would remain!'

The least thought of the dog made Magpie's eyes laugh. He loved that biter big-time, I tell you, and the foxy dog loved him back.

'Come in,' Magpie invited, and I followed him past the wooden water barrel and the grey-blue flagstone, past the small table with its plaid-patterned oilcloth, along the cracked stone floor and down to a big, ruptured armchair.

'Plant yourself there,' he said, and I sat down.

'How's the Dad?' he asked.

'Oh, no loss on him,' I replied casually.

'Tearing away like an old coat,' he said, grinning.

He was fond of my Dad. And then he looked at me closely. 'Were you in the wars, lad?'

'Oh that. Just a scrape,' I said, dismissing the few scars. 'They're hitting at me a bit in school, that's all.'

'I'll wager they're in the wrong, too,' he said gravely. And then he brightened. 'And what brings yourself? Surely not the card-playin'?'

He moved to the dresser to get me a drink before I could answer. A bottle of stout, which he poured at a slow tilt, until the glass wore a black waist and a creamy head. I sipped. Pure poison. But I acted as if a drink of stout was nothing new to me. He opened a second bottle for himself, which he slugged by the neck. I watched his bony Adam's apple moving as he drank.

'Too early for the drop of *poitín*,' he said. 'I keep my own still, of course. Just so I can rely.'

Raw whiskey. And illegal, too. But Magpie was a law unto himself.

'I was wondering about the planes flying around,' I said. 'Everyone is.'

'If everyone asked me, wouldn't they know,' he responded, wiping his thin face with the palm of his hand. 'Haven't I drawn them planes over to me, away from your side?'

'And why are they here?' I asked, impatient.

'Profit's the why they are here,' he said.

'Profit?'

'Yes. They're scouting for treasure. Prospecting. They're making maps of the land. Close-up squints of every little hill and nook. And I've come on fellows out yonder,' – he pointed past the one kitchen window – 'down on their hunkers with a big box in front of them. They put a drill in place a few days ago. It looked nothing much. Just a very tall tripod, or the skeleton of a big tent, with a ladder up agin' it. But it was taking samples of rock just the same.'

Then he nodded meaningfully at me, and fell silent. I waited, fully expecting him to continue. But he didn't. Instead he took another slug from his bottle. I was supposed to understand what his words meant!

'Samples of rock,' I echoed, hoping to restart him.

'From far under us,' he said at last. 'We're sitting on a goldmine, Paul, and I'm afraid they've found it now.'

I was surprised but I didn't share Magpie's fear. As a matter of fact, I was thrilled! A goldmine! It was almost as if I myself had found the goldmine. I couldn't think why, but then and there, without another question, I wanted to take the credit for it. Nor could I hide my excitement from Magpie.

'You ain't dismayed?' he said, looking at me closely for the second time.

'No,' I answered. 'It's a kind of wonder, isn't it? The idea of a goldmine, I mean.'

'That's a natural enough reaction,' he replied. 'But I'm fearful, just the same. Come on and I'll show you the why.'

We arranged to walk back across the Callows together, after Magpie had 'equipped' himself by putting on a pair of wellingtons. I stood at the door of his galvanise shed while he went in to get them. There seemed to be an entrance from the orchard side, as well.

'Can I go into your orchard?' I shouted after him.

'Hush,' he said. 'In there's the blossoms. And do you know, Paul? Blossoms love quietness. The people in the Spice Islands now, they grow clove trees. And they nurse them trees like babes wrapped in swaddle. They whisper an' croon aroun' them, just to make the blossoms happy. And I'm thinking, there's a lot to that attitude. Their trees produce mighty cloves. And my trees produce powerful apples.'

I had all but forgotten about the goldmine. Magpie seemed to be able to weave a spell to make you forget the big, obvious things. He told me he'd been a gardener once, for the people who had owned a mansion there, long years before.

'The bloodline dried,' he said. 'The last, a decent woman, upped and departed. The house fell to ruin. Its stones eventually went to pave my haggard, or some of them did. I managed to preserve the apple orchard. Not a whit else. Only the apple orchard.'

I didn't ask to see the orchard any more, because now there were tears in Magpie's eyes. It bothered me to see him upset, but later I got to reasoning that a man's bound to be sentimental about lost things when he's as old as Magpie, things which might quite easily make him cry.

'At some future date,' he said, clasping my arm, 'When the blossom-roots have tightened into apples, then you'll see...'

I swear I didn't understand him even four-eighth, as he himself might have put it.

❦ ❦ ❦

Riff-raff regarded me as unbiteable, now I was with Magpie. He ran along ahead of us, through the Callows, sniffing everywhere he went.

'I can see a path,' Magpie said.

He was surprisingly agile, especially when we came to the 'give' in the ground. The Callows country suited him.

'I can see several paths,' I told him.

'Some of them could lead to your sudden end,' he warned. 'No, the path I see ain't mapped, as such. It's in my head, more'n anything. And it wends. It ain't direct at all.'

Because of Magpie's 'path' we took a long time to cross the Callows, often going sidewise, sometimes even going back over our own footsteps. I thought this absurd. Magpie believed it was necessary for our safety. And it did lead us to a blackthorn thicket containing two pheasants, a brightly plumed male and a drab brown female.

'Shush!' said Magpie, stooping to his knees. 'Look at the

pair of 'em. Ain't that a marvel now?'

The male was perched on top of the female, and his beak seemed to be biting her neck. They were mating, but I played innocent.

'What are they doing?' I asked Magpie. 'Fighting, is it?'

'They're continuing,' he said quietly. 'They're continuing on.'

And that was as much as I could get out of him regarding the two pheasants.

'Why would you be fearful about the goldmine?' I asked, after we had moved farther.

'Look about you, and you'll see the why,' he said.

'You mean these Callows?'

'They'd be ruined by the goldmine. Such terrible pollutants would descend into them. Flow and descend.'

He leaned slowly down and carefully broke off a rush-stem. There was a creature living on top of it, inside a silken pouch. Magpie fingered the pouch and this golden-brown spider leaped out onto his palm, then spun round and round, a giddy ball.

'She's the only gold I give a damn about,' Magpie croaked, casually flicking his open hand. 'She and all the wild hereabouts. Do you see that, Paul? Do you see what I mean?'

'I do,' I answered, just to placate him, because I didn't see really. Given my choice of spider or gold, I'd pick gold any day. Well, probably I would. But I did love the Callows, maybe not as deeply as Magpie did, but then he was so much older, and I was only just getting to know them. I hinted as much to him. He chuckled, then he said as much back.

'You'll grow to value them yet. It's in your nature.'

We had reached Keaveney's Quag by now, and he made

to turn for home. The sun would set soon, and he told me he didn't like to be abroad in the Callows after dark. I thanked him for the walk, and we said our goodbyes. Then I remembered something that had been bothering me for a long time.

'What does the word 'Callows' mean?' I called after him.

'That,' he shouted back, 'would be 'river meadow', from the Irish word, *caladh*.'

River meadow. What a wonderful name! As I watched, Magpie receded into the darkening landscape, with his dog Riff-raff bobbing ahead of him. Then I turned. Our house lights were already on. The sight brought a sudden hurry to my bones.

3

Facing the Enemy

'I THOUGHT WE HAD REARED YOU BETTER!' Dad exclaimed.

He chewed me up for having crossed to Magpie's without leave, and Mam set about eating the pieces. But the news I had to tell bought me a respite.

'There's going to be a goldmine in Darkfield!'

They seemed doubtful, especially Mam.

'A ruse, on your part,' she said, eyeing me closely. 'Or else another of that Magpie's famous tall tales.'

'He's seldom wrong,' Dad countered, and for a moment they were frowning at each other. But then, recollecting themselves, both turned to scolding me again. 'No TV' was the end-result, followed by 'Up you go to bed.'

I lay awake in the twilight and began to think about Cora's idea of power words. I figured that maybe you could start a spell just by saying a certain word. Not any old word. You had to have a power word. I began to think that if, for instance, you say 'Fire!' with exactly the right amount of alarm in your voice, everyone runs. Or suppose you say 'Autumn', a mellow word, summer ends there and then – even if the sun is still fairly high in the sky – and autumn breaks over the world. I can't prove this, of course. Nobody can prove magic. But it's a theory of mine still. And I began to believe that I had found my own power word at last. I'd used it already to help soften the blow with Mam and Dad over my Callows escapade. I whispered it to myself now.

'Goldmine!' It possessed a strange resonance. Suppose I was to say it in public – I mean outside home – I might start a rumour that would fly in all directions at once, throttling to death every other rumour about the coming of the aeroplanes!

The trick was to pick the best spot from which to unleash my power word. If I chose well, the glory of its spell would come back to me on the double. And just as I was falling asleep, the best spot stole into my mind.

❦ ❦ ❦

'Sir, you were wrong about the map-makers,' I gently informed Mr McGrane, early next morning in the classroom.

'What? Who spoke just now?' he blustered, raising his head from the roll book that he was totting. There was a complete, open-mouthed silence, and shock registered on every face. *Nobody* ever told Mr McGrane he was wrong.

Cora kicked me on the shin. 'Shut up! You'll get us all in trouble,' she whispered.

'I found a power word,' I whispered back.

She just kicked me harder. Overkill, that was Cora Delaney's style.

Mr McGrane stood up from his desk. The pulse on the side of his face was whipping at a fair pace. And the silence rose even over the yellowed, dog-eared maps of Ireland and Europe that were haunting the high walls.

'Gold, sir,' I said. 'The planes have found gold in Darkfield.'

'*Gold?* You're raving, boy. Who told you that?'

'I have it on the best of authority, sir,' I said grandly. 'But I can't name my sources just now.'

'Sources indeed!' He seemed bewildered. He didn't know how to handle the idea of his favourite pupil saying such defiant things. 'Your head is full of dreams, Pauly Duggan. Get back to work at once. It's far from gold you were born.'

The teacher wasn't the only one who didn't believe me. But at least my classmates *wanted* to believe. They milled around right through break-time. Raymie Boland and his crew hovered at a respectful distance. I enjoyed being the centre of attention. More so even than was usually the case at home. I felt like Captain Valour again. All I lacked was the cloak. All I needed to say was 'Goldmine!' The power wouldn't wear out of that word, no matter how often I repeated it.

'What's yer sources?' Boland jabbered at last. 'Tell us or I'll bate the name out of ya!'

'How many of a gang will you need this time?' I asked, standing chin to chin with him. His long upper teeth bit his lower lip. He eyed me uncertainly. No doubt I looked different, on account of the power word.

'See this fist,' he said, raising a pudgy mitt – more for show than anything else, I could tell. Pad Burns stepped between us then.

'Leave him, Raymie,' he said, sounding sensible for once. 'We'll wait until the start of the holidays to see if he's bluffing or not. He must know something if he gave all that guff to McGrane.'

'He's all blow, like a sheet on a clothesline,' Boland spat derisively, turning away.

Right on cue, those terrible twins, Hynes and Dervan,

did their little duet.

'Who's sentenced?' Hynes said.

'Pauly's sentenced,' Dervan replied.

'Death sentence!' both of them said together.

But nobody was interested today. I held the crowd in my thrall. And there was a fresh stir in the schoolyard that morning, an excitement that made feet pound harder and throats shout louder and hearts beat faster, solely because of me. I could sense the spell beginning, gathering up little gaggles of children and sweeping them along on its reckless odyssey.

But not Cora, alas. She seemed angry with me again.

'See,' she said, as we walked home from school. 'See what you've got yourself into now.'

'My power word's genuine,' I assured her.

'And I suppose your Magpie O'Brien is to thank for this goldmine stuff. He saw you coming, a bigger fool than himself. And he made up this goldmine just for a bit of glamour.'

'He's dead against the goldmine, in actual fact,' I said.

'Did he show you one shred of proof that there is a goldmine?'

'Well no, but I believe him. We have an understanding, Magpie and me.'

Cora promptly crossed to the other side of the road. She said I could take this as a sign that she and I had used up all *our* understanding.

As the days went by, I began to re-evaluate. I felt a bit isolated now. I'd gone and shot my big mouth off, and the Captain Valour notion began to grow more and more hollow. Nothing for me but to keep faith with Magpie's words, and hope that somehow, before the first of July and the start of the summer holidays, the rumour I'd started would prove to be true.

As a matter of fact, it did. Well, half-true at least. Definite news came out of the radio, and pictures filled up the TV. Darkfield, the small rural village where we lived, was rich in deposits of lead and zinc, and even of silver. But there was no gold, and somehow this information saddened me for a day or two.

'My power word's dead,' I told Cora.

It was the weekend on which the news of the mine became public, and I dreaded going back to school. Raymie Boland's gang might feel that they still had some unfinished business with me.

'They're into picking on others now,' Cora said. 'Girls, as well as boys. Did you see what they did to poor Martina Moore? Threw her in the river, ruined her good clothes.'

'I saw it,' I admitted. 'But her own brother did nothing. And he's in Sixth.'

'Afraid to do anything, like the rest of us,' Cora concluded. 'You see, Paul, the truth is, they don't need an excuse for bullying.'

I began to feel badly about the overall bullying situation, not just my own. But Monday went well. Mr McGrane said we should be very grateful indeed that there wasn't going to be a goldmine.

'Cyanide,' he said, 'is what gold-mining companies use – the world's worst poison! It strips the gold from the common rock. Darkfield will have its share of pollution, boys and girls, make no mistake. Silver, lead and zinc are no angels, any more than you yourselves are angels. But gold, gold is the very devil incarnate!'

He sounded like the wizened preacher in that TV series set in the Wild West, one episode when gold was discovered, but the children complimented me during break, clapping me on the back and saying how wise I'd been, all along.

'I was half-right, I suppose,' I said, acting all modest and winning even more backslaps as a result.

'Ya were half-wrong,' Raymie sneered. 'Keep yer predictions to yerself an' yer mouth shut a'from now on, Pauly Duggan.'

'He's getting mild,' I said to Cora, later. 'Soon he'll be a pussycat.'

We both laughed. Cora had a real hearty laugh, a big plump laugh, though she herself was skinny as a sally rod.

❦ ❦ ❦

Everything began to change in Darkfield. 'The world has discovered us at last,' old John Hobbins proclaimed. He had one foot in the grave, and probably knew it, but he didn't let that stop him from dancing a jig of joy over news of the mine.

'And will you profit from the mine, old John?' Dad asked him.

'No more than yourself,' he said. 'I'm a few acres too far south. But still, isn't it a blessing? It's nearly as good as winning the county final, I say.'

Old John wasn't the only one who felt the commotion. Everywhere I went, the song sounded much the same. Questions and exclamation marks on everyone's lips, and stars bedazzling every pair of eyes. *Isn't it well for the young? No more exile! Can you imagine? Our own industries! But do you think it'll last? What! There's enough metal to keep us digging for two lifetimes!*

It seemed everybody had latched on to the strange, new-fangled power words. The Mine! Bonanza! The

Lucky Strike! Even Father Burke, our parish priest, got caught up in this fuss. He urged us to hold dear our traditional values of kindness and caring and decorum, while at the same time referring to the coming development of the mine as 'God's generous intervention in the affairs of Darkfield'.

I thought of Magpie. The only unhappy man in my village. I intended to visit him soon, to see if he had changed his mind at all. But film crews had begun arriving, and of course we found ourselves following them around. I went with Cora, Ted Connaughton – a boy whom I had become friendly with in a formal kind of way – and others, to the shops and the crossroads where we knew the crews would be stationed. With us came some of the attention-seeking adults! Magpie vanished clean out of my mind.

We were let fiddle a bit with some of the cameras and other equipment. All looked so alien, so space-age, there among the green fields of our village, that the Wise Woman said: 'Will the cows ever give us their blessed milk again, after seeing these strange contraptions?' Gradually I began to weary of the mine idea. I wanted to be shut of the cameras. I retired to the Callows for peace.

The hay meadows billowed, free of floodwater. The marshy tracts had shrunk somewhat, but were dangerous still. The corncrakes had arrived, unseen, and begun to breed. You'd almost imagine that they had never been away. Except that now their harsh calls would often keep you awake at night. Their chicks hatched, and the hay meadows hid these scraggly little creatures well. One day I managed to catch a glimpse of three chicks. Then I saw a hooded crow, circling. He would drink eggs or gobble down chicks – mercy and he knew nothing about each other. The grey-streaked lapwing eggs hatched also, and I heard the alarmed cries of the lapwings themselves as that hooded crow landed.

Sure there was blood and death, but still the Callows provided a sanctuary for birds, whatever the season. Dad had given me some of the names – pipit, moorhen, whooper swan – and Mam purchased a pair of binoculars through which we could watch from the Callows' edge. It was hard to gain a good vantage, because the land lay flat and low. It might not look scenic, especially on an overcast day, but the Callows teemed with life. One afternoon, Dad and I saw maybe thirty swans grazing together.

'A herd of swans,' Dad said.

'No, Dad,' I corrected him. 'A herd applies to cattle.'

'Aha!' he exclaimed, frightening the swans. 'I have you now!'

It pained me afterwards to discover he was right. A herd of grazing swans is what we saw.

I didn't forget my devil's coach-horse. He worked a little mine of his own, under the boundary stone – a series of tunnels made by other insects, and for all I knew maybe some of these other insects became his food by times. I learned from him, as from the bird-life of the Callows, that there's this great elaborate web which attaches us each to all – but I didn't stay long enough to work it out properly. Such a job might take an eternity. And I seemed only to have a moment. The giddiness had got into my bones. I couldn't enjoy the quietness now. The cameras drew me back to their bland, unblinking gaze.

One night our faces appeared on TV. My own, Cora's, Raymie's too – he continuously pushed in. Our fringes and short haircuts and summer freckles and wide-apart ears and grinning gap-toothed mouths featured on a news segment about the young people of Darkfield – but we weren't asked any questions. There were only our faces crowding on top of the camera, and a big 'Yaaay!' at the end. We scarcely recognised ourselves.

Our houses, too, looked strange, on account of the aerial shots the film crews took. Were chimney-stacks really like that, with pots and wire on top of them, and twigs roughly shaped to make jackdaws' nests? Were slates so steep, gutters so drab and dusty, gables so proud?

Our fields on TV resembled the tiny fields of a toy farm belonging to Cora, except that their animals – miniature cows, sheep, horses – all really moved. But one sight remained absolutely unmistakable: the great rolling Callows which divided our village in two, the *wet meadows* where native herbs flourished, where stunted blackthorns held firm, and where butterflies of rare casts and colours silently tumbled.

And as I looked at the Callows on TV, I felt proud somehow, prouder than I did of the coming mine. For the Callows were more magnificent than anything a human being could make. But I will admit, I was mixed up, distracted by all the hot-air talk, the cameras and the strangers come to Darkfield.

❦ ❦ ❦

At school there was a different kind of excitement. At first I didn't notice. I had taken my eye off Raymie and his crew. Could you blame me? I was enjoying some peace from them for the first time in ages. The one thing I didn't want was to draw Raymie on myself again. That's why I looked away mostly.

But I couldn't keep shutting my eyes to the rough treatment he gave to others. It upset me to see younger boys and girls crying after Raymie's gang had cornered them, though I wouldn't have admitted as much. And I felt guilty, too. I had a recurring dream of Captain Valour rescuing children, but in the dream I was always running the other way.

Cora felt as badly as I did, maybe worse. She was small and thin, and sometimes Raymie or one of his thugs bumped into her 'accidentally on purpose', so she felt shaken and intimidated. Their apologies afterwards were all a screen against her mother, the Wise Woman. Power words could be made powerless, I realised.

My blood began to boil. Slowly. I thought and thought, but meanwhile the bullying continued. The gap between the Captain and myself grew so wide that we could have been mortal enemies. Except that I wasn't even a super villain. That 'honour' belonged to Raymie. I was a super-zero.

Raymie became more and more showy in the lead-up to summer. Each evening he, Pad Burns, Hynes and Dervan would saunter into the crossroads shop owned by Tommy Hodgkins – not to buy a pennyworth of sweets, as the rest of us did, but to stuff themselves with whole cans of sweets, and full blocks of ice-cream. Where did they get the money? They didn't have florins or half-crown pieces as you might expect if they had got them at home, but pennies and ha'pence – stacks of small coins jingling in their pockets, heaped onto Tommy Hodgkins' counter, traded for lavish amounts of sweets and confectionery.

'Are ye sure this is all your own now, lads?' Tommy would ask, scratching his orange mop of hair.

'Oh sure we're sure,' Raymie would reply. 'Honest money fer honest sweat.'

Then he and his cohorts would laugh and throw shapes,

and pretend to be gunmen come to rob Tommy Hodgkins. When he got used to the idea, Tommy knocked a great kick out of it altogether. In the end, of course, Raymie would get out of hand, and Tommy would lose his temper. He probably thought he had done his duty, though, just by asking them about the money. He didn't seem to suspect anything, otherwise.

But I began to suspect. Raymie had always been short of money until now, or 'skint', as he would say. My second reason for being suspicious was that I noticed very few youngsters calling to Tommy's shop anymore. The gaggle of kids going in for penny sweets had dwindled to a trickle. Cora and I still went in, as did Ted Connaughton and some of the fifth and sixth class lads, but hardly anybody else. Except for the four jokers, of course.

Things came to a head one hot evening in early June. I saw Raymie collaring another lad, Joe Whelan, and my antennae bristled. I saw the coin switching hands. I saw the upset look on Joe's face, the tears beginning to brim, and I spoke out. Without planning to – the words just seemed to say themselves.

'I saw you.'

'Ya saw nothin', Pauly Duggan.'

'I saw you taking Joe's money.'

It was too late to step back from the situation now, but something sang in me – a glorious feeling that I was invulnerable, that Raymie couldn't touch me.

He leaned close to me. He blinked. His pals gathered round, but I looked only at him.

'C'mere Joe,' he said then, pulling away. 'Tell this gobdaw! You gimme the money, right?'

'I gave it,' Joe told me, looking down.

Raymie had his arm about Joe's neck, loosely. He

squeezed a little, laughed.

'Why did you give it?' I asked Joe.

'A present,' Raymie said, squeezing again. 'Right, Joe?'

'A present,' Joe repeated hopelessly.

A big circle of children had gathered round us, drawn by the prospect of a fight. 'Raymie gets lots of presents,' Pad Burns said.

'Are ya soft or what?' Raymie shouted at him. ''Course I don't get lots'a presents.'

I felt the chance begin to slip from me, so I went for broke.

'Don't take any more presents,' I said, 'from anyone.'

And then at last he said the two little words I had been yearning to hear for a long time.

'Make me.'

'All right,' I answered, and the feeling of invincibility charged through my blood.

I swung. A neat left-hand hook! It caught Raymie full under the mouth; he stared at me for a moment, then slowly his legs buckled, and he sank onto the warm tar road.

'C'mon Raymie! Get up!' Pad and Dervan urged, clutching him under the oxters. But Raymie wasn't rising.

'A rag doll,' Cora said later, 'would have more kick in it than Raymie.'

But there was still work to do. Raymie's pals. Surely they would go for me. They looked as if they were thinking about doing just that, but then a strange thing happened.

The circle of watching children started to close in on Raymie. Slowly they shuffled forward, chanting quietly 'Give it back, give it back.' Raymie stirred. Next moment Ted Connaughton, who always struck me as being fair-minded, stepped forward and said: 'Hand it over, Raymie.'

He fluttered his open hand in front of Raymie's face. Raymie lifted from his drowse. He slowly turned out his trouser pockets. A big scoop of coins spun onto the road. Raymie got fully to his feet, shrugged off his mates, kicked ineffectually at the coins.

'Stick 'em,' he snarled. 'I'm goin' home.' And off he dundered without another word.

Ted Connaughton picked up the coins. 'Put up your hands anyone who is owed money,' he said.

Several hands went up. The money was shared out. Not every raised hand got a coin. There seemed to be a shortage. We all knew where to look. Raymie's pals. They had no choice but to empty their pockets, just as Raymie had done. Again the money was distributed. Soon it would make its way to Tommy Hodgkins' shop, but this time spent by those who were entitled to spend it.

❦ ❦ ❦

Raymie Boland didn't try to get back at me, though there was always the fear that he might. For now the zap seemed gone from him. No, Raymie did his best to keep away from me, and so did his friends. Even the two clowns, Hynes and Dervan, didn't play their chanting game at my expense any more.

But this behaviour was too good to last. As June wore down to the summer holidays the gang became active again, drawing money from children whom they knew wouldn't tell anyone. But they had become secretive, more careful, and they no longer spent the loot in Tommy Hodgkins' shop. Leastways, not on the walk home from school.

I heard complaints from a few children who had been made to pay off Raymie. I talked to Ted Connaughton, for he had heard whispers, too. Someone should do something, we both agreed. Only Ted wasn't a fighter, and I didn't relish the idea of taking on Raymie again. My win began to seem a fluke, a lucky blow, born of frustration – and Raymie wouldn't be such a soft target in future. I told Cora as much.

'Fighting would solve nothing now,' she said. 'Maybe we could get everyone to warn off Raymie.'

I asked around. Nobody was knocking the house down with enthusiasm. The Sixth Class children were due to finish with Darkfield School for good, in a few weeks' time. Raymie, being in Sixth, would finish too, surely. So they said, anyway, and from the way they said it I could tell their thoughts were elsewhere already.

I asked some Fifth Class children. 'What bullying?' they asked. They hadn't seen any. I must be imagining things. 'Show us proof,' one said. 'There'll always be some bullying,' another conceded. 'The world's not perfect. But it's small fry now, just relax, ignore it. Raymie won't be here in September.'

A few weren't nearly so civil. They actually accused me of being a glory-hound! Fine thanks after all my efforts on their behalf! They probably wanted a quiet life, but didn't we all?

So June ended, with no action taken, and school stopped. I looked forward to a summer free of the old oak desk, the pen with its sprained nib, the white porcelain inkwell. I'd swap the sarcasm and peeling green walls of Mr McGrane's classroom for the leafy outdoors. I'd see Cora now and then. I'd visit Ted Connaughton's house. He and I had become friends. No more Raymie Boland fouling up my radar. Goodbye, pencil-case and stale lunchbox. Hello, eternity of summer, my time to be footloose!

Leastways, that's how I imagined it would be. Hadn't it always been that way before? Why change a winning idea? But Dad called me aside one morning in early July and said: 'You're old enough now to lend us a hand on the farm. There's work to be done, you know. Some people around here might be making fortunes out of selling their land to that mining crowd, but for us there's the hay to save.'

'The Callows, is it?' I asked.

'No. Those meadows always take longer to grow, on account of the flooding in spring. We'll save the Callows hay next month, if the weather holds. It's the Fort Field and the Old Tillage I'm talking about now.'

Dad had names for all his fields. One was called Smoothing Iron, another Santy's Stocking! Don't ask me how or why they got those names – it had happened long before Dad's time. And as for the Callows, well, leaving them until last was Dad's way of giving the corncrake and other wild birds a chance to rear their young undisturbed. Our cows loved the sweet hay meadows of the Callows best of all, but if the fields flooded, they would have to live with the loss. It was a risk Dad always took, which left him doubly eager to secure the ordinary hayfields as soon as the initial spell of fine weather came.

So I got my first real introduction to those two back-breakers, the pitchfork and the long-handled rake. I helped turn the long swathes of freshly cut grass so that their undersides seasoned in the sun. I learned how to make hay-cocks and how to bind them against the wind. I raked the fields clean of stray stems. My hands blistered, and my bones ached. The back of my neck reddened. I was in no mood for fun.

Mam complimented me, and well she might. For hadn't I taken on jobs that were hers to do previously. There was just the three of us, Mam, Dad and me. Our pony, Jack, pulled the mowing machine – on whose high tin seat Dad sat stately as a lord, watching the meadow fall in gentle swathes under the blade. When I asked him for a go, he said it was too dangerous. I didn't sulk, though. Not even when I saw Mam sunning herself in the back garden, her housework finished early, and with free time on her hands for once. I felt pleased, almost, to see her wave happily out at me.

Jack the pony was a lifesaver, the way he could pull that ancient mower, the huge trams of hay he could gather. Dad let me lead him off to the Callows when he had unyoked him after a day's work. I would hug his neck while he snuffled at me through hot, breathy nostrils. I'd ride him bareback over the higher parts of the Callows, which had grown firm under the sun's blaze. I'd cling to his mane for dear life, and feel the refreshing breeze against my face, and watch the ground flow away underfoot. Then I'd lead him to the pasture known as Catherine's Mead, and set him free. He'd bound off a good few paces, pick a soft patch of grass, and tumble there for all he was worth, his four legs kicking up at the sky. It was his way of ridding himself of tiredness. Mine was simply to go to bed early, before the sun had even properly set.

As I grew more used to the work, I began to stay up longer. We'd watch TV in the kitchen. The newly discovered mine was still making the headlines. Local people were interviewed. It was like watching a soap opera where all the characters were from Darkfield! The men all said how great it was that there would be work for them in the mine. Most were poor and could barely survive on their small farms. Some were gleeful because they'd be able to sell their land to the mining company and get a high price.

One of these was Raymie Boland's father. 'I'm on the pig's back,' he said, throwing his cloth cap into the air.

'Oh, the old devil,' Mam said, feeling peeved. 'Isn't it the likes of him that would get all the luck?'

'I'll never hafta do a tap a'work again,' Boland Senior bellowed blithely, and his laugh would wake the dead.

'You never did a tap of work in your entire life!' Dad shouted at the flushed-looking face onscreen. But I was thinking that this could be a godsend. Maybe Raymie Boland would move away from Darkfield for good...

'Ah hardly,' his father said just then, in answer to the interviewer's question, and my fervent prayer was dashed. 'We'll hardly move, like. Don't my fambily belong hereabout. Where else would we get such fine neighbours...? '

Then the women came on. They joked that it would be fun to meet all those fancy American men who were due to arrive in Darkfield.

'It'll make a welcome change from the dull type of man we're used to!' Pad Burns' mother said, laughing.

'They shouldn't make such a display of themselves in front of the whole nation,' Mam said solemnly.

'I'm glad you don't feel the way them other women of Darkfield feel!' Dad responded with a grin.

A politician came on with two glints for eyes. 'Good times,' he chuckled. 'Nothing ahead but good times.'

Then, since he was Minister for some government department or other, he tried to act cool and dignified, but his enthusiasm kept getting the better of him.

'Darkfield will be the biggest lead and silver mine in Europe,' he told us. 'It also contains significant deposits of zinc and cadmium and tin. I want to state quite categorically to you tonight that Ireland is rich in mineral resources!'

'Are you happy to see outsiders coming to operate the Darkfield mine?' the interviewer wondered.

'Most certainly,' the politician said. 'We need international expertise to run the mine.'

'Tax-free?' the interviewer quizzed, edgily. 'With ninety-five per cent of the profits going abroad? Don't you think we are being rather generous, to say the least?'

'The mining company has ploughed huge amounts of money into this venture already,' the politician said with a cough. 'Their technical skills are needed, since we lack these in our own country. And think of the benefits in employment...'

Everything seemed to be happening in a hurry, as far as the mine was concerned. The mining company had purchased nearly all of the ore-rich land. They were putting up 'No Trespass' signs where everybody had had right-of-way until now. They were wheeling machinery in. Soon they would commence production. Those were the exact words their executives used. 'Soon we will commence production.' Nobody had ever uttered such awesomely important-sounding words in Darkfield. But we were so busy between saving the hay and whatnot that we honestly didn't pay much heed at first. Leastways, I didn't.

It was high summer, the time when all of nature seems so full and in its prime that you'd be fooled into thinking things would stay like this forever, with no development or change.

Then one night, Magpie O'Brien was interviewed on TV. It startled me to see him there, close-up, peering out at us from the box. It brought a pang of guilt to my heart. Dad grew all excited, hugging his knees and telling us to shush until he heard what his friend was saying, though he himself was the only one making any noise. And, give him his due, Magpie spoke well. But what he was saying caused Mam and Dad to shake their bewildered heads. He was saying that the mine was bad news. It would do more damage than good, in the long run.

'Open-cast mines, they're the ruination of many a place,' he argued. 'What else would they be? Don't they break the mould of nature so it'll never fit back together again? Open-cast means they'll clear the surface – houses, trees, haggards – they'll eradicate the very grass itself, they'll clear all the clay. It ain't a word of a lie I'm tellin'. And then they'll scoop the minerals out. And leave a poisonous hole after them. And Darkfield will never heal. Not in twenty lifetimes of wishing. That's what they'll do, now. Unless we put a stop to them.'

Magpie cast his gaze to the ground and plucked a marigold, which he then placed behind his ear.

'This is wealth enough for me,' he said, and I was reminded of the golden spider in the silken pouch. 'I won't be selling, though I'm right in the spot where the richest seams of minerals sit.'

'You are? How do you know that?' the interviewer asked, with a smirk on his face.

'Oh, I know of old,' Magpie said mysteriously.

'But wouldn't you enjoy the money?' the interviewer said, taking a softer tone. 'Couldn't you hit off for a foreign holiday, buy a new house, even marry perhaps?'

'I been married all my life,' Magpie replied. 'Married to these Callows. I'll fight for them accordingly.'

But the interviewer cut him off there. The camera panned slowly over the flat flower-filled Callowlands, along the white walls of Magpie's cottage, past the iron railings of his gate, and upward to include the high orchard branches festooned with young apples. We three stayed silent for a while. Then Mam said: 'I wonder if he's in earnest?'

'Oh, he is,' Dad replied. 'I know by the set of his jaw.'

'He won't be very popular,' Mam said. 'My heart bleeds for him – the poor good-natured creature. They'll say he's standing in the way of progress.'

'They will,' Dad agreed. 'He'll brazen it out, though. He's tough as an old goat. He's the sort who won't give in.'

Both of them were concerned for Magpie. The idea of him berated by everyone troubled me, too. And the fact that I hadn't visited in a long while made me feel even worse. I lay restless that night, listening to the sharp yelp I knew to be a fox's, out amid the wilds of the Callows, and thinking of Magpie.

4

Two Challenges

THE HAY WAS SAVED. We waited for the hurry to leave Dad as it always did at this time. Soon he would become his old relaxed self. This summer he would be able to tell me that I, too, should take my ease. We had caught the fine spell. The winter fodder would be good. It was all a matter of luck, but Dad invariably took the credit for having picked just the right time.

'I can tell these things,' he would say grandly. 'I know by the sunset, and by the way the midges fly. I can read the signs better than a weather forecaster can.'

'Oh, listen to him,' Mam would laugh. 'The chancer! Taking after that Magpie fellow.'

But this time Dad didn't relax, or make the usual comments. Instead, he said, 'It's a shame about the Callows. I have a feeling about them this year.'

'He always has 'a feeling' about the Callows,' Mam joked, nudging me.

'Is it the mine?' I asked. 'Will the mine kill the Callows? Magpie says it will.'

'I don't know that, and neither does Magpie,' Dad said. 'I've a feeling, though, we'll lose the cut of the Callows meadow this year.'

'Is it floods you're afraid of?' Mam asked. 'The big river is as low as I've ever seen it.'

'Just you wait, my girl,' Dad cautioned. 'Tomorrow will rain and rain.'

He was right. The rain came next evening. It bucketed down, and indeed it would never properly clear for the rest of the summer. People who had been late in cutting their meadows suffered as a result. They could only watch their hay rot slowly into the ground.

'Pauly, it's as bad as it could be,' they'd say when I met them on the road or at the shop. They sounded so ill-humoured that it seemed they were adding the y just for spite.

'The name's Paul!' I'd snap, feeling cheated because my summer was dwindling away, being washed out as drizzle followed downpour.

'I'm tempted to pack it in, Pauly,' they would declare, ignoring the niceties of my name. 'Farming's a dead loss. When that mine opens, I might look for a job there.'

But still, through rain and disappointment, I felt the urge to visit Magpie nagging away inside my head.

'Dad, I'm going across the Callows,' I said, one morning.

He must have heard the determination in my voice, because he didn't argue. 'You're big enough to go on your own, aren't you?' he replied, as if I had been reluctant about it or something. Dad was like that. He could turn the tables on you in an instant.

I hit off for Magpie's cottage. When I came to the Callows boundary, I turned over the heavy oval-shaped stone, just to check on my devil's coach-horse. I wanted to see if the rain had affected him. But there he was, healthy as ever, the same tube-body on him, the same quivering antennae, the same evil-looking tail. He was harmless, as

I've already mentioned, but boy was he ugly as well! 'No wonder he hides all his born days under that boulder,' I said to myself.

The Callows presented me with various expanses of fresh water. We referred to these as loughs. The wading birds might cherish them, but Dad's Callows hay was surely done for. I splashed cautiously across. And where the hay meadows with all their late, waterlogged flowers – red clovers and ox-eye daisies and yellow rattles – ended, the marshy lands unfailingly began. They had turned thin-skinned once more on account of the rain, and on account of the big river over-spilling its banks. The tall flaggards and rushes struck against my knees, drenching my pants, flicking droplets of water into my wellingtons. I staggered and squelched. The heavy socks knitted for me by Mam soon were soaking wet. I took detours around the quags and the deeps.

I met a tiny new frog. He hopped onto the snout of my wellington and stayed there happily for a good few paces, until a lodged rush swept him off. He probably liked the slick wetness, I decided. And round about were marsh marigolds and any amount of ragwort and sedge. Water spiders gliding on the silver pools. Cool characters waiting for a midge or a fly to fall in. Water-beetles weaving wonderful figures-of-eight, only to submerge themselves when I dipped a finger in their little pool.

The Callows could keep me forever if I let them. I forgot about time passing when I walked there. I stayed respectful of them, and I came safely out the other side.

Over the years, many a creature had failed to do so. We'd lost sheep to the mire. We'd even lost milking cows and prize cattle. They had fallen, never to rise again. I liked to think that Jack the pony was shrewd, though. He was well used to the Callows, even if temporarily confined to Catherine's Mead. He would be let range freely again when the Callows meadows were saved or, as seemed more likely now, waterlogged past the point of saving. He didn't once lift his gaze, but I knew he was regarding me as I walked past. Probably hoping that this wouldn't be another workday.

Eventually I came within reach of Magpie's gate.

'I discerned you a mile off,' the old man said as I climbed over. 'I knew the gimp of you, I did. I watched your progress.'

'I meant to call sooner,' I told him.

'Have ye the hay saved?'

'We have. Except for the Callows.'

'Ah, that explains your delay. Ye're lucky, being one of the few. But the Callows hay won't be saved this summer, take my word.'

'I saw you on telly. You're a brave man, standing up for yourself.'

'I ain't brave at all. I'm a coward, in actual fact.'

That took me by surprise. Magpie could puzzle you with one simple sentence. He was complex – or deep, as Dad called it. Deep as Keaveney's Quag.

'You haven't sold, have you?' I said, wondering if he had changed his mind.

'Devil a sell. Didn't I tell you I'm a coward!'

'How is that, if you haven't sold?'

'I'd be afraid to sell. Too many big consequences to selling. Sure, this is all I know.'

Magpie went on to describe how two representatives from the mining company had paid him a call.

'They carried black leather cases. Inside was a slip of paper for me. The things that pass for money nowadays! It contained a one followed by four noughts in its little window. Them lads have money to burn. But I tore their cheque in two, and handed the pieces back. They weren't so pleasant then. They said I'd come round, eventually. They were wrong there, too.'

He invited me in, and gave me tea from a cracked mug. He had a blaze dancing in the hearth. I sat beside it, in that old armchair of his with the guts showing, and silently sipped my tea, staring into the laughing flames, the red mosaics of turf. He favoured the stone hob, on account of the miserable weather. He was a noisy drinker of tea, was Magpie. He tended to slurp. Otherwise we stayed silent for a good spell. Then I heard the crickets under the stone hob, piping their song. I asked about them.

'I don't know how they got there,' he answered. 'They're a mystery, same as anything else that's living. They're at home in the ashes. That's what gives me hope. Them being at home in the ashes. And when I throw the ashes out, sure they're still in here.' He half smiled. 'The world itself could be thrown out, or turned into ashes, and they would still be here.'

I saw what Magpie meant. Leastways, I thought I saw. The crickets somehow stood for endurance. I told him about my pet devil's coach-horse, surviving under the big stone.

'Ah, the devil's coachman!' he exclaimed, using that insect's other name. 'Some people would say I'm him!' He let a pleasant cackle, his thin chest quivering gently under the neat black waistcoat.

'Where's Riff-raff?' I wanted to know.

'He's sentenced to the shed for a while. I tell you he was trying to be friendly, but didn't he nip one of them mining people in the bum, and though it was comical to see, I can't have him being thought discourteous by visitors.'

Magpie was deep all right. Deep as a spring well.

Soon he started mooching in the bottom drawer of his old wooden dresser. He came up with a stack of large white pages, which reminded me of blotting paper, except that these looked smoother, finer. There were drawings on each – made by some kind of pencil, I assumed. I couldn't see properly, nor did I fully dare to look, because Magpie seemed anxious to shield them in next to himself. Then he placed them on the oilcloth-covered table, pencil-marked side facing down.

'I'm decided on making a stand,' he said, looking flushed. 'You'll think me foolish, no doubt.'

'A stand?' I said.

'I'm opposin' them mining people. I can't just let that monster roll over us. I have to stir up the locals.'

'You'll have a job,' I told him. 'They're all giving out about what you said on TV.'

'Even if I change a few around to my way of thinking,' he replied, 'that would be a start. I must make up some slogans now, against the mine.'

'At least it's not a goldmine,' I told him 'Mr McGrane says a goldmine's the worst.'

'No mine's a good mine,' Magpie said solemnly. 'Least of all an open-cast mine. You might as well peel the flesh off your own face and expect people to recognise you afterward. That's what open cast does to the earth, Paul, it peels off the face.'

I had barely recovered from the shock of these words when I got a different kind of shock.

'Signs,' Magpie said, handing me one of his paper rectangles. 'Signs of life.'

I turned it over and was amazed to see a large picture of a wading bird, lovingly sketched. I recognised it by its extraordinarily long bill.

'A curlew,' I said.

'The same,' he replied.

'You did this? It looks real as anything,' I told him.

'A poor imitation of what lives in them Callows,' he shrugged. 'Here's some more signs.'

He passed the stack of papers over to me. 'They're posters,' I said, thinking of the giant colour-sheet of Captain Valour which adorned my bedroom wall.

'Posters?' he queried. 'Is that what they're called now?'

I studied each in turn. A wild goose, a corncrake, a frog leaping into Keaveney's Quag, a rare Callows flower called 'Summer Snowflake', an orchard – which I recognised as Magpie's own – a snipe, a red shank, and more besides. All magically drawn by Magpie's hand.

'From my observations,' he said. 'And I've left a gap above and below each, do you notice?'

'I do,' I told him.

'To allow for the slogans,' he informed me. 'To talk the mine down.'

'Can I help you with the slogans?' I asked.

'Sure you can! Are you a good printer of block letters? We want people to be able to see these from twenty paces.'

'I'm a reasonable printer,' I said, feeling nervous at the prospect of ruining his wonderful artwork.

Reasonable was good enough for him. He found two black marking pens and we set to scribing, one at either end of the table.

TADPOLE POND OR TAILINGS POND?

This slogan went with the frog sketch. Magpie explained that the mine would wash its own poison in what was known as a tailings pond.

SAVE OUR LANDS; SAVE OUR LIVES.

We put this under a general sketch of the Callows.

PURE FRUIT? OR POISONED?

This suited the apple orchard drawing.

The wildflower sketch made us think up:

DON'T TRADE FRESH AIR FOR LEAD DUST!

We worked on into the evening. Our heads ached from thinking.

When we had finished with the slogans, Magpie said it would be necessary to preserve the posters from the rain and such. He found some transparent plastic sheeting, and we used that as a kind of envelope. It was all very crude, apart from the lovely drawings, but it was a start.

'I'll have to travel now,' Magpie said, 'to deliver these aroun' the locality.'

'To people, do you mean?'

'No; to places where people gather. I'll go on my bike now.'

'I'll go instead,' I told him. 'I'd be quicker. Tell me where to put these.'

He was delighted. He gave me a list of suitable places. Then he gave me twine to tie the posters around tree-trunks and pillars.

'If I had the money, wouldn't I produce these professionally in town,' he declared. 'They'll have to do, homespun as they are. But first and foremost, be sure to tell your parents what you're at.'

Then he got an old satchel to carry the posters in, and strapped it onto my back, and sent me on my way with sincere thanks.

'You're a brave lad, Paul. Don't get drowned, whatever you do.'

Brave? I didn't think there was anything brave about putting up some posters. Anyone could do it. But I had undergone a change without realising as much. I had begun to take Magpie's side with regard to the whole idea of the mine. It seemed natural to be on Magpie's side, I told myself as I sloshed through the Callows. It felt good. He was an underdog, after all. Fighting the mighty publicity machine of the mining company, and the tide of opinion in Darkfield, with only artwork and twine and transparent paper as his weapons, and though it seemed hopeless he didn't give up. I was battling enemies of a different kind – but at least I had made a stand against Raymie and his gang. I was an underdog, same as Magpie, same as Captain Valour had been in one story, the one where he temporarily lost his superpowers.

I made my way homeward, sated, virtuous. When I neared home, I had an unpleasant surprise. Who should be standing at the Callows boundary but a knot of young fellows – Dervan, Hynes, Burns – and in the middle of them, Raymie Boland himself. All were soaking wet. They considered it a sign of toughness never to wear an overcoat. Raymie was clutching a cigarette between thumb and middle fingers of his left hand. He was of course the last person I wanted to meet, and the last person I expected, balancing there on the very stone under which my devil's coach-horse lived, rocking it so much that I began to fear for my pet insect's life.

'Is it schooldays?' Hynes asked, seeing the satchel on my back.

'Pauly's schooldays,' Dervan replied, and Pad Burns laughed his unpleasant laugh.

'Shut up,' Raymie told them. 'Evenin' Paul. I'm come fer a chat.'

'Nothing to say to you,' I responded.

'Ah, hear me anyway,' he said. 'I'm come fer to make a business deal.'

'Not interested,' I said coldly.

'Thass what I like about ya,' he said. 'Ya've got guts. A defiant streak, like. An' seein' as how I'll be spendin' another year in that bleddy school, I was kinda thinkin' we could hang around, yerself an' us.'

'No chance,' I told him. 'You're still into hitting on fellows – and girls – smaller than you. You were at it right up to the holidays, and there's still some complaining about you.'

'I could polish ya off here an' now,' he said. 'If'n I wanted.'

'Four against one. You have your cronies with you. I don't have mine.'

'I don't give a rattlin' pin about them niceties,' he sneered.

'My Dad's not a million miles away,' I bluffed. 'And besides, only a coward would do it your way.'

'I'm no coward!' he shouted. 'Every gobdaw in Darkfield knows fer instance I'm the road snoozin' champ.'

'So what?' I said. 'It's an eejit's game, road snoozing is.'

He drew a last drag on his cigarette, and flicked it casually from him.

'I challenge ya,' he said then. 'I challenge ya to a road snoozin' contest.'

The three stooges smiled. 'Raymie Boland challenges ya,' Pad Burns proclaimed. 'Now, Pauly!'

'I want nothing to do with it,' I said, turning for home. 'It's stupid.'

Raymie grabbed my arm, suddenly earnest. 'If'n yer in,' he said, 'I guarantee the rights-of-way to all them childer at school. No money an' no more messin', ha? If'n ya can prove yerself fit fer a road snoozin' challenge!'

'Who's the coward now, Pauly?' Pad Burns said. 'You'll never live it down once we let the word out.'

'A chance to save all them childer, Paul,' Raymie persisted, eyeing me closely. 'Take it or leave it. I'll drop the messin', honest! I swear it on me solemn oath!'

'Even if I don't win?' I said.

'Sure, Paul. Long as you take the challenge. We'll put on a show fer them kids, you an' me, then we'll call it quits, regardless a' which one wins.'

'Why?' I asked him. 'Why do you want to do it?'

He motioned to the three stooges to push off before answering. Seemingly he didn't wish them to hear.

'To repair meself,' he said quietly, after they had complied. He sounded altogether genuine. 'It's the only way. That punch you floored me with was a sucker blow. I weren't expectin' it. So it did damage, I admit that. An' when so many kids saw me goin' down...'

He shook his head sorrowfully at the memory. 'But if'n I bate ya in a road snooze,' he said, suddenly brightening, 'I'll be repaired. I won't be a sucker no more.'

That sounded plausible enough. His image as the local tough guy was important to him. Going along with the road snooze could make my life a lot easier. Not just my life, but other kids' lives as well. And with school about to restart soon, and with Raymie set to attend for another year...

'I'll let you know,' I said, at last.

I had enough to bother me without road snoozing, just now. Magpie's posters still had to be delivered and displayed.

'Game ball,' Raymie said.

Something about the way he said it set off a tiny fretting in my head. I told myself not to take up his challenge. But then the truculent voice I also knew to be mine began its whispering campaign: 'Don't be classified a coward!'

Between the two courses of action, I was in a complete bind.

I should tell you that road snoozing was a game played by fellows who thought they were brave. Braver than the ordinary person who just went about minding his own business. And maybe they were. It was certainly a dangerous game. And Raymie held the title of champion, the specialist road-snoozer.

I'd seen him lie on the tar road and wait for a car to come. He'd lie there until the last possible moment, and he'd be blindfolded so that he couldn't see the car. He could only judge its distance by the sound of its engine. And at the last moment he'd get up and bolt across to the safety of the roadside.

Then the other boy, his challenger, would try to do the same thing when the next car came. There'd be an umpire present to judge the exact closeness of the car at the moment when the player got up. I'd seen cars come to within ten feet of Raymie before he gave way. Nobody else could show the same kind of nerve. He always won and, as is the way with such things, he was admired for his lunatic skill.

❦ ❦ ❦

'Where did you get the satchel?' Mam asked, when I got home.

'Off Magpie. Look what he's made out.'

I showed the posters to her and to Dad.

'He's an artist,' Dad said. 'An artist, pure and simple.'

'He is,' Mam agreed. 'What's all that business about tadpoles and tailings ponds?'

'It's Magpie's way of desisting the mine,' Dad said.

He meant resisting, and I actually corrected him.

'Aren't you getting very big for your boots!' Mam said. 'Speaking to your father like that. And tell us, while you're about it, why did the Magpie fellow give them drawings to you?'

'I'm...delivering them for him,' I said tactfully.

'Where are you delivering them?'

'Oh, this place and that.'

Then I fastened the satchel onto the carrier of my bike, and breezed out the garden gate.

'I hope he's not getting mixed up in all that mining business,' Mam said behind me to Dad.

'At his age? Hardly!' Dad answered back.

The rain fleeced me but it was all in a good cause, as I travelled the rounds with Magpie's posters. To the church gates, the pub, the hurling club, and elsewhere besides. I arrived in with the last poster to Tommy Hodgkins' shop on my journey home. He placed it before him on the counter, and studied the artwork for a while, pinching his bushy eyebrows as he did so.

'Did you draw this at school?' he asked finally. 'It's very nice.'

Everybody knew that Tommy Hodgkins hadn't an artistic bone in his body, but any praise was high praise, coming from him.

'No,' I said. 'I want to hang it in your window.'

'Now you know well I can't do that. I'd lose custom, you see. A lot of my customers would be looking to sell land to the mining company, or to get jobs there, and I don't want to fall out with them. Tell you what! I'll hang it if you tear off the words. It's a fine-looking fox.'

'It needs the words,' I told him. 'I'll hang it outside on that big beech tree there.'

'Ach, you won't,' he said, getting heated. 'I couldn't

have that around the place at all.'

'That tree isn't yours,' I told him, making for the door.

'I'll tear it down!' he shouted after me, getting into a temper. 'You may as well bring it home with you now while it's still in one piece!'

Instead I climbed as high as I could, right up where he would never, in a month of shopping days, be able to reach. The tree dropped water on my face, and the water fed down my neck, but, undeterred, I tied the poster to the whitish trunk, making sure it was angled to catch every pair of eyes that passed the road.

Triumphantly I cycled homeward, pausing only to smile at Tommy Hodgkins scowling at me through the window of his shop. Outside the church I saw a small group of old people, gathered around the poster I had fastened to the gate. They were leaning in close and tracing the drawing (of Riff-raff in a Callows setting) with their quivering fingers. They had forgotten to unfurl their black umbrellas, and the rain fell unnoticed on their bare white heads. *NO MINE IN DARKFIELD!* the top of the poster said. And beneath the close-up of Riff-raff's face, with its attendant rush stems and blossoming flaggards, *FOX CRIES FOUL!* was plainly captioned in my own hand.

5

Making a Difference

THE POSTERS GOT PEOPLE TALKING – I mean differently from before – about the mine. They made people hesitate for a few moments at least, if only to wonder who might have drawn them!

'And I hear tell you're an artist now, Pauly,' old John Hobbins said. 'I'd love to see your paintings, only I can't see a stem.'

The posters actually changed at least one person's mind – the Wise Woman's. That is, if it ever needed changing.

'I must go down now,' she said, 'to view the wild Callows and the beautiful scenery. Lame and all as I am, I must go.'

'Didn't you often go before, Mother?' Cora said.

(They were both at our house. Mrs Delaney and Mam loved to chat.)

'Yes, Cora, I did – to save the hay and to look for certain plants. But now I'm going just to wonder, just to see the pheasant and the corncrake. Who can say how long they'll be left to us, the poor creatures.'

I persuaded Cora to come along with her mother, Mam and myself. Mam and Cora linked Mrs Delaney. It took ages. Mam talked about the lost hay meadow, and the loughs everywhere; Mrs Delaney clicked her tongue in sympathy. I showed the devil's coach-horse to Cora. Delighted that Raymie Boland's weight on the boundary stone hadn't squashed it forever.

'Whatever keeps you amused,' she said airily, 'but I prefer the bright colours of nature to the gloomy ones.'

'There's nothing gloomy about that devil's coach-horse,' I assured her.

'It lives under a stone, doesn't it?' she said. 'It hates the light.'

'Heaven, for a devil's coach-horse, is under a stone,' I argued.

'Hell, more like!' she exclaimed. 'Where else would you expect to find a creature with that name? Give me flowers any day instead. Or butterflies.'

'Flowers or butterflies!' I mocked, annoyed at her attitude. 'You'll have a long wait.'

In fact there were flowers everywhere around us. The deeper you went into summer, the more the Callows showed their colours. Pink orchids, yellow bird's-foot trefoil, purple vetches, cream meadowsweet – these were among the wildflowers Mrs Delaney stooped to caress and name. They lived just above the flooded parts, and about them several types of grass and oat grass crowded.

In the marshy places I myself could identify sedge and rush, yellow splashes of marigold, creeping buttercup and bentgrass. In the drains and streams numerous plants – which none of us could name – floated or stood to the waist in water, so that overall you encountered several habitats side by side, lapping and shading into each other, when you walked our Callows.

We stopped not far from Keaveney's Quag. 'Oh, that blasted mire!' the Wise Woman said, pointing. 'It nearly brought us great misfortune. You know, Mrs Duggan, I blame myself for Cora's accident there. I should never have left her untended. I was too busy picking my herbs, I suppose.'

'All's well that ends well,' Mam reasoned.

'Cora's an able dealer,' I told Mrs Delaney. 'No likelihood she'd fall in today, is there?'

'And you, Paul,' she said, choosing to ignore my joke. 'I believe you go all the way across to Magpie O'Brien's house on your own.'

'I do,' I said bashfully. 'He's an artist, Magpie is.'

'Among other things,' Cora muttered.

'If you like butterflies and brightness so much, why can't you act more cheerfully?' I scolded. She just pulled a long face, bearing out my argument.

'Too bad people don't appreciate Magpie's work,' Mrs Delaney sighed.

'Oh they do!' Mam assured her. 'It's the talk of Darkfield.'

'I'm afraid I saw his beautiful fox picture torn up outside the church last evening,' the Wise Woman told us. 'And I hear the same thing's happened all over. They set fire to the drawing of his that was in the pub, you know, and that uncouth Mr Boland lit his cigar with it.'

'Raymie's father,' Cora said, as if I needed any such reminder. 'He thought it a great joke.'

The news of Magpie's desecrated artwork sickened me to the heart. Then I felt the familiar anger rise. Mam glanced at me sympathetically.

'You did your best, Paul,' she said. 'But what's happened, I'm afraid, is often the way things go when there's a clash of ideas.'

'No!' I protested, not wanting to quietly put up with the situation, but the Wise Woman had begun talking again, and Mam and Cora were paying attention only to her.

'If they were common election posters, I wouldn't mind,' she said. 'But such beautiful drawings! Why can't people agree to disagree with that artist, Magpie, and let his drawings be?'

'Because they're greedy for gold!' I exclaimed.

'Silver, lead and zinc, don't you mean?' Cora put in.

'Same difference!' I said angrily, then took off towards Magpie's house, leaving all three of them dumbfounded in my wake.

❦ ❦ ❦

Magpie's reaction to what had happened to his posters surprised me greatly.

'I ain't bothered,' he said. 'I ain't perturbed in the slightest.'

My mouth fell open. 'But...'

'That's only Phase One,' he explained. 'Our campaign's only beginning, Paul. Will you accompany me on Phase Two?'

I said yes, of course, and we decided to embark on Phase Two the very next day.

The mining company had already laid a roughly pebbled road, out by the far side of Magpie's house, so that their machines could gain access to the ore-land. Magpie had a second bicycle, which he lent to me. We walked the two bikes a distance over this new road.

To either side of us the clay was heaped, the blackthorn bushes upended. Huge yellow bulldozers squatted in some fields. And the fields themselves wore a dishevelled look. At first I was puzzled. Then I understood. The fences had all been ripped out and unravelled. Stakes, gates and dry-stone walls left an aftermath of linear tracks and bare patches of earth. Tyre-marks snaked everywhere, and tall tripods stood at intervals, where the first samples had been drilled.

Magpie and I continued walking our bikes in silence. We saw no cow or sheep or horse to left or right of us. It struck me that even the birds had stopped singing. How could they sing? There was no standing hedge or bush or tree for them to sing from. Only the strange tripods offered height, and these would be more likely to frighten birds away forever than to set them singing.

'It looks a right mess,' I said eventually.

'The mess will get worse,' Magpie replied. 'The strangers are tightening their grip. After the geologists and prospectors, we have the sample drillers. Some use diamond drills to bore down deep, others work bucket drills – it all depends on the placement of the rock. Oh, they know what they're doing, all right.'

We turned the bend and came to a farmhouse. 'That was Paddy Dyer's place,' Magpie told me. 'He was the first to sell. His house is empty now. They'll level it, one of these days. Paddy won't mind. He's moved west, out by Ballybrit – him and his missus, all their kith and kaboodle.'

'A friend of yours?' I asked.

'My nearest neighbour. Reliable in an emergency, though never a card-player, good, bad, or indifferent.'

Soon we passed Raymie Boland's house. Its chimney smoked. There was no sign of Raymie absconding to Ballybrit or anywhere else, though his father had also sold ore-land.

'Should a person take up a challenge?' I asked Magpie.

'That depends,' he replied, 'on the challenge itself, and what's to be won or lost.'

'Well, supposing a person can solve some problem by taking up a challenge,' I told him. 'Not just for himself, but for others as well.'

'What problem are you alludin' to?' he asked.

'Bullying.'

'And what's the challenge?'

I told him about Raymie and the proposed game of road snoozing, and he was upset.

'There's a mean streak in that lad,' he warned. 'It follows on from the Dad. Don't associate, Paul.'

'But didn't you tell me once that the world's made up of tiny patches of land, and that we each have to look after our own? Didn't you say that if we don't look after our own patch of earth, there's no point in talking about saving the great rainforests and such?'

'That's the why I'm concerned for our Callows. That's the why you are, too, I suspect. What other patch of land would you be referring to?'

'The road I walk every day,' I said. 'To and from school.'

When Magpie didn't answer, I sneaked a look at him. His face appeared troubled. His eyes fastened on mine sadly, yet not reproachfully. 'We're both the same kind of fool,' he sighed, after what seemed an age, and my heart sang. I felt that he had just paid me the highest compliment. Saying no more, we climbed our bikes and hit off along the new, roughshod mine road, he travelling at a snail's pace, me zigzagging so I wouldn't overtake him.

We hadn't gone very far when a strange rumbling noise reached us. A rolling and clanking sound, from somewhere out on the main road. 'Dismount,' Magpie ordered, as the first machine came into view. It looked unremarkable – an outsize lorry of sorts, with the words *Darkfield Mining Enterprises* emblazoned on its forehead in red lettering.

'Will we stand in front?' I asked, fretfully thinking of our campaign. 'Will we block it off?'

'Do nothing of the sort, child,' Magpie instructed. 'Let it pass peaceably through.'

Then came a bizarre-looking vehicle – tall as any tree – with pulleys and cables and ladder-like steel rods, and a cab affixed to one side of the engine. There, a man in helmet and dungarees sat. The man saluted, and Magpie saluted in return. Magpie was too placid, I felt. He always took good manners too far. We had to keep close to the roadside, lest the articulated steel threads crush us as they rumbled forward.

The giant machine was followed by a series of lesser ones, some with excavators and drills, more with broad shovels to the front. Then came cranes, and trucks laden with barrels and other equipment. Tall lorries hauling huge trailers passed. I heard them growl in low gear, heard the scrunch of stones under their many twinned wheels. The occasional stone shattered or flew. Sometimes a driver would roll down his windscreen and say, 'Hi kid', but I never answered.

On and on the strange machines trundled, slowly convoying past us. Some resembled gigantic, incredibly long racing cars, except that they had tractor-shaped front portions, and chunky tyres that were designed to cope with depths of muck. We gaped. I doubted if even Magpie, despite his wide knowledge of the world, fully understood this mechanised invasion. For my part I imagined an army of aliens, come to claim the flat, defenceless fields of Darkfield.

We waited there by the side of the road, with our old bicycles yanked across us, until the mining equipment had passed. We had no choice but to wait. It took an hour, maybe more. Magpie scratched his head, bewildered.

'They're landed sooner than I thought,' he said. 'No doubt they mean business – but so do we.'

It seemed an unequal battle. Even Captain Valour would probably have given up the ghost in face of such opposition, but I never said. Magpie looked disheartened enough without that kind of talk. We got silently on our bikes and started Phase Two of our campaign.

We stopped at each house, being now well away from the mine site, and tapped at each door. Magpie had a list of blank-lined pages – a petition – which he talked about and asked each person to sign. And each person read aloud the petition at the top of the page, slowly, there on his or her doorstep.

We, the Undersigned, strenuously oppose the establishment and operation of an open-cast lead, silver and zinc mine in the village of Darkfield, due to the hazards said mine would impose on the health of our people and animals, and on the wellbeing of our unique Callowlands.

Such-like jargon, cumbersome but clever. When they had finished reading, each person, bar a few, gave a little shake of the head, and handed our petition back unsigned. They wanted to talk only of the convoy, the spectacle, the company now known as *Darkfield Mining Enterprises*, and we had no power words to match these.

'Thank you,' Magpie said, all decorum, at each refusal. I, of course, was fuming.

As the day progressed, I took to muttering under my breath. I kicked the odd stray path-stone out of my way. I left the occasional gate unclosed. Once, provoked by a man who swore at Magpie and told him to go drown himself in his snipe-ridden Callows, I swept the head off a garden rose.

'That,' Magpie told me quietly and sadly, 'is the act of a

vandal.' And I felt ashamed.

But then, on the odd occasion when we got a signature, Magpie would grin at me and shake his shoulders with pure glee.

We travelled well beyond Tommy Hodgkins' shop, and on the return journey we went in. Magpie bought me a bottle of lemonade, and a straw to sip through. He handed the petition to Tommy.

'It's been a fair scatter since we saw one of them around here,' Tommy said, handing it back. 'And I'd say it'll be a fair scatter before we see one again.'

'You're such…' I began, but Magpie cut across me. 'There's a first time for everything,' he said to Tommy, then we went outside.

'Who put that up there?' he asked, pointing at the beech tree. 'Was it yourself?'

I looked and – yes, my poster was still broadcasting its message, silently but surely, to the passing world.

'Up Riff-raff!' Magpie chirped. 'Up Riff-raff!'

That put both of us in good spirits. And at the end of a long, heartbreaking day, some tonic was badly needed. We had thirteen signatories. Three of them had even told us that they'd been persuaded to change their minds by some wildlife posters they'd seen, a few days before.

'Come in to meet Mam and Dad,' I coaxed.

'I will – but only out of deference to our friendship,' Magpie said. 'I ain't going in to petition, mind. And there's one other condition.'

'What's that?'

'You'll keep the bicycle. I have enough in one. I don't require two.'

I agreed, of course. To say no would have been a grave insult.

❦ ❦ ❦

Dad was charmed by Magpie's arrival, dancing every attention on him. Mam was slightly less enthusiastic.

'You seldom call,' Dad said, after pouring him a stiff whiskey.

'Don't yourself come over to me,' Magpie answered. 'And this lad is a great help. We been on the campaign all day.'

'Well and good, if it keeps him out of trouble,' Mam said. 'He's forever getting into scrapes.'

'We encountered them mining machines,' Magpie said. 'They'd frighten you, to look at the unnatural shapes of them. What mind could design such abominations? Instruments of torture would hardly be worse.'

'Abominations and instruments of torture,' Dad repeated, seeming to enjoy the sounds of these words.

'I have the bike for a present,' I told Mam.

'He won't lack for a pastime, between the bike and the pony,' Mam said by way of thanks.

'Which pony do you mean, Ma'am?' Magpie asked, momentarily befuddled.

'Don't you remember the pony you brought for Paul when he was born?'

'Ah yes,' he said with an endearing smile. 'That's 'im I see regularly. The Callows pony.'

'You were on TV.' Mam said

'So they tell me. I've no box. No juice in the house at all, as a matter of fact.'

We knew that 'juice' was Magpie's word for electricity, and 'box' his non-existent TV.

'Candlelight!' Magpie said. 'I manage by candlelight. It'll do for the few years I've left to me.'

'Haven't you ages left in you yet?' Dad said. 'A reader, a cyclist, a healthy man?'

(I fully intended to ask Dad about the significance of reading where a person's life expectancy was concerned, but the moment slipped past.)

'I might be rooted out of it,' Magpie replied. 'There's many would like to see me cleared.'

'Over the mine business?' Mam said. 'It's unjust, but people have their own ideas, I suppose.'

'I wouldn't mind if they had their own ideas,' Magpie asserted. 'They're not let have their own ideas! They're bombarded by the powers that be. They're told what to believe, and it ain't for their own good either.'

On and on the chat meandered. Magpie sipped his whiskey intermittently, and I mostly listened. Mam and Dad seemed to agree with Magpie, though they still had sympathy with the people who hoped to gain a decent living from the mine. When the entire confab threatened to become a bit complacent, I decided to intervene.

'Here,' I said to my parents. 'Sign our petition.'

They seemed winded by this request. And Magpie stared at me, aghast. But both of them signed. Magpie told me later that I had committed a second act of vandalism in one day, by putting pressure on them to sign.

'It probably won't do much good,' Dad said as he handed Magpie's pen back. 'Ye haven't many signatures. How many do I see there at all?'

'Fifteen,' Magpie said, 'if I include the two of you. We must have met more than a hundred people today, but fifteen's no bad return.'

'No bad return at all,' Mam and Dad agreed, looking at him doubtfully.

❦ ❦ ❦

Magpie decided to hold a meeting. The venue was the local hall. The meeting was open to everybody, and about thirty people showed. Darkfield Mining Enterprises were invited to send a representative, but no word came back from them. Dad and I attended, but Mam didn't go. Nine of the people who showed had already signed the petition. The one person Magpie didn't expect to attend was the parish priest, Father Burke. He and Magpie were enemies, but they always behaved civilly towards each other.

'Will we see you in church on Sunday, Magpie?' Father Burke joked, with a broad grin, as they shook hands.

'No, priest, nor the Sunday after,' Magpie answered, smiling back at him.

Eventually the meeting started, half an hour later than planned. Magpie had delayed in hopes of even more people attending, but when he did speak, he spoke from the heart. 'The earth is made up of patches of land,' he said. 'You have your patch, and I have mine. We are answerable to our patch of land. I feel answerable to the Callows that adjoin my house. There's no place like them. They contain wonders. They contain the hoarse bird of summer nights, the corncrake. I ain't slept a wink with him yet. Wouldn't you think I'd be accustomed by now? But every summer he comes from his travels, and insists on talkin' 'bout them to all and sundry. Goin' *craak! craak! craak!* all night. I love the creature, but he ain't no poet, is he?'

Everyone laughed at Magpie's interpretation of the corncrake. Perhaps they thought he was mad, but at least they laughed. Soon he turned their mood around, so that they became quiet, even sad-eyed.

'Near nightfall I hear the curlew, saying his own name. I

watch his big arched wings gliding, when he allows me, which is seldom. I owe a fortune to him for all the good health he's brought. And when I see the snipe flying in big circles above, I know I must step carefully because I'm near the nest. Then again I'm visited by them fine grey geese from Greenland by times, whose laugh does me a power of good. Through spring I do enjoy watching the plover gradually turn golden-backed after being the drab scut all winter. But just when he's golden, he ups and leaves us. Then there's the redshank; he's a piper. There's the lapwing. He's brave when the hooded crow descends...'

The Callows were Magpie's element, and we all sat enthralled. He talked of salvation then, for all the creatures of the Callows. He urged us not to let the lights of rare flowers be quenched. He even drew down Keaveney's Quag.

'That's a deceptive spot,' he intoned. 'Didn't I near disappear there myself as a boy. Only for the flicker of lightning on the water, only for the intervention of the heavens themselves, wouldn't I be drowned?'

'The intervention of the heavens?' Father Burke chuckled loudly. He was in favour of the mine, and had waited for a chance to trip up Magpie. 'I never knew you were a believer?'

'Whether I am or I ain't don't matter!' Magpie answered truculently. 'That's not the why we're here. Aren't we here to discuss the mine? If the fate of the world depends on us alone, and I believe it do, shouldn't we be all the more conscientious about how we behave toward it?'

'The world is God-made,' Father Burke said. 'The fate of the world depends on God alone.'

'I don't expect God to intervene,' Magpie argued back. '*We* are the keepers. The world is in our own poor hands.

But if we don't have a care, Darkfield will be blighted forever. It will fall into the wrong human hands – those of the power grabber and the greed merchant. Sure, it's happenin' even as we speak.'

Magpie made a few new friends by virtue of his arguments, but he also made enemies. Arguments flew back and forth. As soon as he called for an action group to be formed several people left, with a shake of their heads and an insult on their lips. Begrudger. Crank. Fool. Seeing him gracefully smile at all the wounding words taught me a sharp lesson. Finally one fellow advised that he should sell his ore-land to the mine 'for the good of your own health'. Dad got fiery and challenged this man to withdraw his threat, but the man just walked out.

The action group was formed – Against Mining In Darkfield, or AMID for short. This group would put its point of view to the County Council, the politicians and the mining company, and it would try to raise public awareness of the harm caused by open-cast mining.

'We'll lose the battle,' Dad said to me as we cycled home. 'The mining company has bought up nearly all the land, and they're paying a hefty penny for it. It's hard to blame the people who sell.'

'Why are you and Magpie fighting if you will lose?' I asked, feeling despondent.

'Because it's worth fighting,' Dad told me. 'And Magpie still has his land. He says that if we fight well this time, we'll help some other village just like ours to win in the future.'

I began to wish for an action group of my own to counteract Raymie Boland. If I could get ten people with me, well, that would be positive luxury. But no, I had only myself. Hearing the debates and the ideas of Magpie and Dad fired me up, though. I paid a call to Ted Connaughton. He advised against the road snoozing option, as I somehow knew he would.

'You can't trust Boland,' he said. 'Anyway, the bullying is not *your* problem. Tell Mr McGrane if you must. Tell them kids' parents, even! But skip the road snooze. It could be the death of you.'

'The kids themselves don't even tell their parents,' I answered. 'So who's going to heed me? And telling the teacher would only bring grief down on everyone. You know how crazy he can get. No, I'll chance going through with it. Just think, every hassle solved if Raymie keeps his word! And he might – he just might.'

Ted was disgusted. Our friendship cooled. But I was inspired by Magpie's example and had become full of a bleak zeal to right the problems of the world. Magpie had shown me how just one person can make a difference. He was my new, unglamorous Captain Valour, fighting – no matter the odds stacked against – to hold on to his patch of ground, and I felt that I could attempt no less.

September drew closer. School would soon resume. I set a date for the road snoozing with Raymie. Ted Connaughton reluctantly agreed to act as umpire. Other children were witnesses to the agreement. Not that it was a legal document or anything, but we had to be sure everyone knew what was involved – namely, that Raymie and Co. would keep their promise.

This had a downside, too. There was a danger that some child would tell Mr McGrane about the contest, and drop us all in the soup. But nobody was fond of him. He ruled by fear, not kindness, and you would be slow to confide in him as a result. Besides, the times were rough and ready. You didn't run to your parents, no more than to the teacher, unless it was dead serious. Sometimes you didn't run even then. I'm not saying that this was the right way. I'm just saying it's the way we lived, as children.

6

The Contest

I BECAME CRANKY AS A BAG OF CATS in the days leading up to the road-snoozing contest. I forgot to do the chores Mam and Dad had left out for me, or I skipped through them so hurriedly that they might as well not have been done at all. Mam decided I needed fresh motivation.

'Your friend, Captain Valour, should be in Kelly's Shop in town by mid-September,' she said slyly.

'He's not my friend,' I replied grumpily. 'He's just a fictional character.'

'A fictional character,' Dad said. 'That sounds mighty impressive altogether.'

'Issue 101, is it?' Mam persevered. 'We'll have to get that for you if you smarten up about your work.'

'I don't want it,' I told her, and in the same moment realised that I was only speaking the truth. I didn't, indeed, want it.

'But wouldn't you miss the great heroics, the adventuring?' she said, taken aback.

'There are enough adventures without making up new ones,' I said. 'Besides, I'm too busy with real life now.'

'Too busy to do your chores?' she quizzed, strapping a thin slice of patience to her voice. I didn't respond. Dad would wait no longer.

'Is it a strike we have now from your lordship?' he asked sarcastically. 'Is it that you're too good for the rest of us mere mortals?'

'I can't understand it,' Mam said. 'He's always been reliable at home, if not away from home. What ails you, child, can't you tell us?'

I couldn't tell. If Dad heard about the road snoozing, he'd blow a fuse. And Mam would forbid it outright. The crux came when I got into a shouting match with Dad over some trifle about herding the cattle, and when I stayed out in the barn half the night as a result, Mam consulted the Wise Woman.

Mrs Delaney arrived in the garden path, her lame step more pronounced than I had ever seen it before. That was a sign that she meant business. Along with her came Cora. Mam ushered the Wise Woman into our parlour where they whispered together. Cora and I had to stay put in the kitchen.

'You're in trouble now,' Cora said. 'Mother is a proper witch when she gets her hooks into a patient.'

'I'm nobody's patient!' I exclaimed. 'No witch will be hooking me.'

'You're in trouble,' she repeated, 'and you're going to land yourself in even bigger trouble. I know all about the road snoozing contest you've set with Raymie Boland. I ought to tell your Mam.'

'Oh that,' I said with an offhanded shrug, though in fact I was alarmed. 'That is a complete joke, Cora. A joke in a very good cause.'

'Explain, please,' she said. 'No fairytales, now.'

I played the entire thing down for her benefit, at the same time stressing how necessary it was for me to carry it through. The joke, I assured her, was that I would jump away early – just entering the contest would do for Raymie Boland. The good cause was that there would be an end to bullying in Darkfield.

'Why are you so uptight if the road snooze is only a joke?' she asked, wagging the hinged crook of her spectacles at me.

'Naturally I'm uptight,' I replied, 'in case Raymie doesn't keep his part of the bargain. We all stand to gain if he does.'

I fully expected her to throw another question, or even to tell Mam about the entire caper, but instead she left down her glasses on the table, and pressed her hair back with both hands, and gave me an adoring look.

'You're a hero, Paul,' she said. 'You're nothing short of a hero.'

I was amazed. I could have whooped for joy at outwitting Cora Delaney with my persuasive powers – no easy thing to do – but suddenly her mother opened the parlour door, and invited me in. I managed a weak smile for Cora's benefit. She smiled beatifically back. And then I grew nervous all over again.

The Wise Woman walked slowly around me, prodding and poking and examining as if I were a coat on a clothes-hanger. Her height changed with each step, and when she finally stopped to regard me, I found it hard to meet her gaze on account of the way her glasses shimmered.

'Eleven years is it, Mrs Duggan?' she asked absent-mindedly.

'Going on for eleven and a half,' my mother answered. 'Isn't that right, Paul?'

I didn't contribute to the discussion.

'Adolescence,' Mrs Delaney said with a sigh.

'Adolescence?' Mam queried.

'We're losing our little boy,' Mrs Delaney said, sighing again.

Our little boy. The very idea made me wince. But Mam's reaction was far more dramatic.

'Oh God, is it that serious?!' she exclaimed, panic-stricken.

Seeing her react so badly, the Wise Woman rushed to console her.

'Good heavens, no!' she said. 'I only mean that your Paul is turning into a young man!'

Hearing this news, Mam composed herself, and hugged me, and laughed at her foolishness. The worry and puzzlement I had caused her were swept away in that laugh.

I told Dad about the Wise Woman's diagnosis myself. I suppose I wanted to get back into his good books. One redeeming virtue of Dad's was that he never sulked.

'We managed all right around here without any of this adolescence stuff before now,' he said. 'I don't see why we should change.'

Then he looked at me sharply.

'Is there any information you might need?' he asked. 'About nature and such?'

'Nature?' I said.

'You know...the facts of...of...of where we come from?'

'Well?' I said, folding my arms and waiting to hear about the facts of life, what everyone peculiarly referred to as 'the birds and the bees'.

I knew about babies, of course. How they got to come about. How they got to be born. I might have been hazy about some of the finer details, and maybe the moment was ripe to hear these from Dad. But he turned everything around.

'Well,' he said back. 'Well, remind me to tell you, won't you? And while I'm on the subject, you've not been very civil this past while. You could show a bit more consideration, you know. To your mother at least. A bit more...humanity.'

Who could make out the motivations of adults? Not me, that's for sure. And besides, didn't I have enough on my plate, trying to fathom my own predicament? To fathom it, and to face up to it?

I had always slept soundly, but now the road-snoozing worry began to toss and turn my dreams. I would wake up in pure dread, and slip onto the floor, scarcely able to put one foot in front of the other. I'd shamble over to the window and wipe a clear patch in its misted glass with my sweaty hand. I'd peer into the big darkness of the Callows beyond. I'd stand there trembling in only my shirt, and I would see nothing.

Night after night, this happened. Then, after a week of nights, I saw lights rising out of the ground. Pale, ghostly lights. I pressed my face to the glass, wanting to be closer to those lights. They rose, and they began to move. Will o' the Wisp was abroad. He danced – up, down, over, back. He was dancing solely for me. The joy of seeing him pierced my heart. I went back to bed. He, the spirit of the Callows, tucked me safely in. I felt reassured somehow that everything would work out right.

❦ ❦ ❦

So August ended, and school resumed. Cuckoo and corncrake left our Callows and headed for the warm south, Spain and Africa, as they had always done at this time. None of us saw them leave. Not even Magpie, though he had kept an unfailing eye out. We just didn't hear them for a spell, and then Magpie said: 'It's safe to pronounce them gone.'

Raymie Boland and I kept our appointment.

We fixed on a straight stretch of road that ran downhill past Darkfield Church. By now many children had got wind of the contest. They hid behind the hawthorn hedges at the sides of the road, and looked on. They didn't want to alert car drivers as to what was taking place. Ted Connaughton, our agreed umpire, would be the one to decide the winner.

At the last moment Cora tried to dissuade me, and when that didn't work, she said, 'Promise. Promise it's a pretend.'

'It's a pretend,' I told her. 'I'll jump away early. For sure I will.'

'Ha!' Boland exclaimed, as she retreated. He had overheard us and now he strutted about the road, talking, talking constantly.

'This road-snoozin's a drag. We'll have to improve it, spice it up, like, for them thass spectatin'.'

'How can we do that?' I asked.

'We'll only snooze fer cars comin' downhill.'

He swung his arm to describe the gradient of the road.

'This way the cars'll come faster. I like 'em fast!'

There was a dip in the middle of the road's long gentle fall. A car would almost be upon us before the driver could see.

'That's not part of the deal,' I told him.

'It needn't concern ya, Paul,' he replied. 'You jump away early. It's purely fer me own intentions, d'ya see?'

Ted Connaughton looked at me for my consent. I gave it by means of a nod. 'I told you not to trust him,' he said, then stepped ten paces down from us to fix the exact snooze site.

A ragged chant rose from the hedges, instigated by Dervan and Hynes and Pad Burns, and taken up by a few others who would do anything not to be on the losing side.

'Creel the Pauly! Creel the Pauly!
There's goin' to be a killin'
Down beside Darkfield Road!
Creel the Pauly! Creel the Pauly!
Pour' 'im in an enamel basin!
Raymie'll make fat puddin's,
Puddin's out of Pauly's blood!'

Just then, I heard other voices – few and hesitant at first, but gathering strength, growing plentiful. *Come on Paul! Come on Paul!* They were shouting for me. Not exactly a massed choir of angels, nor indeed a highly inventive school of poets, but they were behind me – they wanted me to win! I thought of Magpie, tirelessly petitioning. I thought of Will o' the Wisp, dancing through the Callows. I took heart.

We tossed a coin. Raymie would go first.

He strode to mid-road. He threw a shape or two, shook his muscular arms and legs, stood to attention, gave one last look about him. A heavy black scarf was fastened as a blindfold, tight across his eyes. I was beckoned by Ted Connaughton to check it. I just waved an arm. I wanted it all to be over and done, and to get away home in one piece if I could.

A line had been chalked across the road. Raymie lay down on his back, saluted theatrically, let his arm fall.

'Be good now, little childer,' he joked.

The road was quite narrow. A car could scarcely swerve enough to pass. Raymie's big lanky shape stayed perfectly still. The silence welled. My heart knocked loudly, yet that silence welled.

We waited and waited. There were never very many cars on the roads. We might have to wait for half an hour, maybe even more. This thought nearly drove me mad. A droplet of sweat rolled slowly, hugely, down my spine. I prayed.

At last! The faint purr of a car reached us from somewhere out of sight, on the high, church side. Our heads turned towards the sound. The contest had begun!

Raymie Boland didn't stir. A black car appeared in the distance, travelling fast. Now it was Raymie versus the car – that loud engine, the wheels closing fast! Behind me, someone screamed.

Raymie was up! He got his feet under him as he was supposed to do. A screech of brakes blended with the scream, but Raymie had leaped, leaped away beyond the shuddering mudguard, to land on his face in a thicket of ferns across from us.

The cheers rose to acclaim him. The startled-looking driver ploughed past, just managing to steady his car. Then he let his horn blare all the way until he had gone completely from our sight.

Ted made a white chalk-mark on the roadside. The chalk had been swiped from Mr McGrane's desk that morning while Boland diverted his attention. There was a gap of about one decent stride between the new chalk-mark and the snooze line which had been drawn earlier.

'That's how I see it anyway,' Ted Connaughton said. His face was white as the chalk in his hand, and no wonder. Raymie had gone within an ace of being hit.

I knew now that I couldn't win. Somehow, this made me calm. I'd go through the motions, give them their show, jump away early, and to hell with what might be said afterwards. I walked out onto the snooze line. All the faces regarded me, a condemned man. The black scarf was tied, and Raymie Boland came to test its tightness.

'More,' he insisted, adjusting it himself until it hurt my eyes.

'Ya'll be right as rain,' he said then, close to my ear. 'Relax yerself.'

Then he left me, and I lay down.

I hadn't long to wait. The silence one moment, then the car. I could just about hear its approach from somewhere towards the church. I thought of the first plane, the mining company's first prospecting plane, and how I had fallen over on seeing it.

But now, suddenly, I realised that Raymie had played me for a fool. The muffled sound in my ears said it all. He had ensured that the scarf was fastened not only over my eyes, but over my ears as well.

I ripped frantically to loosen its grip, but could not. How can I tell you the panic of hearing only the muffled din, and knowing it was getting closer, and not knowing how near or how far it was? I can't, that's the truth. But my body told that panic to itself. It grew rigid as a crowbar. I willed and willed, but my body wouldn't move. The screeching, tearing din bore down on me and I could do nothing but wait for the death that must come.

Silence, then. More complete than all the fearful silences in Mr McGrane's classroom, rolled into one. But a silence that was born of peace, not of fear. 'Death's not so bad,' I thought.

Something cold touched me. The chrome fender of a car, if I'd only known! Hands dragged me upward, tugged the black scarf off. 'Thanks be to Christ you're still in one piece!' the driver gasped, as my eyes met his. It was Tommy Hodgkins, the shopkeeper. Round about, in a big circle encompassing me and him and the car, twenty, maybe thirty children stood staring down, all the schoolchildren of Darkfield Road. I gazed at their silent, hovering, concerned faces.

Now Tommy Hodgkins recognised who he had in front of him. His ginger eyebrows quivered, the way they would do when he was calculating the cost of Mam's groceries. Maybe he even remembered the poster incident, for his relief switched to anger, and he gripped me by the ear.

'I might have known!' he said. 'You're a certified blackguard, Duggan, and by God your father will be told!'

He lugged me into the back seat of the car, giving my ear one final painful twist for good measure. Then he slammed the door. I glimpsed Cora's face, staring after me in horror as he shunted the car in gear.

❦ ❦ ❦

Mam and Dad were dismayed. They apologised to Tommy over and over. It made me feel terrible, the consequences of my action. Tommy kept scolding and criticising. He talked of 'chastisement' and of me 'suffering from a swelled head', by which he meant I was overly proud. Nothing Mam or Dad said seemed to be enough for him. He ranted and raved, and wouldn't leave it be.

'I hear you,' Dad kept saying. 'I agree with you. It is shocking conduct. I agree.'

'You're raising a criminal,' Tommy said finally, 'a juvenile delinquent.'

Dad drew the line at that. 'Paul's nothing of the sort,' he told Tommy with a hard edge to his voice. 'And now that you've said your piece, there's the door.'

Tommy Hodgkins shut up at once, and walked meekly out.

My pains were only beginning, however. I was amazed to find myself despatched to bed without another word. Mam and Dad must have been so stomached that they didn't know what to say anymore. I heard them whispering, below. Then I heard sobs. And I knew – I had shattered Mam's faith in me. I had broken her heart.

The morning breakfast was a cold silence between my parents and me. Neither of them looked in my direction. They couldn't bear to look, I suppose. And when I arrived at school, hadn't Tommy already told Mr McGrane of my misdemeanour.

'Just name him, Pauly,' Mr McGrane said. 'Just name the boy who put you up to this. Who else was involved?'

'I did it myself, sir,' I answered.

He would request, and I would make the same answer. He went high and low, he paced and stood still, he coaxed and threatened, but I held firm.

The entire morning passed with me stood before Mr McGrane, being interrogated. A courtroom drama on TV had nothing on it. I was kept in for both breaks. Then I got another shock: a policeman arrived.

Mr McGrane hastily told me to sit down. Cora gave me the same distasteful look as she'd given to my devil's coach-horse, then averted her head.

The policeman lectured us one and all. I kept thinking that he'd call me for further questioning, but he scarcely glanced in my direction. He rocked gently on his feet and seemed, in fact, to be focusing on a spot slightly above and beyond our worried heads. His voice was deep, abrupt.

'There'll be no more of this road snoozing in Darkfield.

Ever! I'll throw the book at ye if there is. Do ye hear me now?'

'We do, Guard.'

'Can I depend on ye to keep safe from that class of conduct?'

'You can, Guard.'

'The good name of Darkfield is in safe hands, so.'

A threat, a cajole, a compliment – then he was gone. Every boy in Darkfield School would want to be a policeman for a few days, but Mr McGrane didn't seem impressed. He shook his head slowly. He gazed at us sorrowfully. The whip in his temple was pulsing hard. He vowed, now that he had claimed the classroom back, to crucify the ringleader – me – for bringing shame to his school.

He started by giving me one thousand lines to write out. 'This is your first instalment, Duggan,' he spat. I would be Pauly to him no more – and for the first time in my life, I missed the y.

'This is your first instalment of humility.'

❦ ❦ ❦

Boland never let on what he had done. He'd been prepared to put my life at even greater risk than the game demanded. He must have known that I realised as much. But if so, he never let on. And though a lot of people had seen the game, this part of it would stay a dark secret between him and me.

'Ya won fair an' square, Paul' he said, already covering his tracks. 'No more money, an' no more messin'. I keep me word. An' no more road-snoozin'! Hell, no! Ya stretched it far as it could go, Paul. The game's dead.'

He spat vigorously on his hand, and grabbed mine, and forced me to shake. Then his gang of three each shook my hand, but at least they didn't feel the need to spit.

It was home time, and everybody was pouring out from the long-windowed, tall-chimneyed school. I shook myself free of Raymie and his crew, and looked for Cora, but she had already fled away down Darkfield Road. I wanted to explain to her about the road snoozing, but instead I dithered.

What could I tell her? Not my usual old guff, that's for sure. Where was the use in putting a twist to everything just for appearance's sake if, at the end of all the twists, you felt just plain bad? And, though the truth mightn't show me in a favourable light, I vowed to tell Cora nothing less.

I started running. She saw me and ran faster. It took the guts of half a mile before I caught up with her.

'Wait,' I gasped, out of breath. 'I'm sorry!'

'Sorry you didn't kill yourself, is it?' she flung back at me, with a sideways toss of her head. 'Some hero. Some pretend.'

'I froze. Honest, Cora.'

That made her stop. She was fit to fall down with exhaustion anyway, no more than myself.

'You froze? You didn't stay there on purpose?'

'No. The fear made me freeze. I'd planned to get away, just like I promised, but the fear got a grip on me and I couldn't move. I'm no hero,' I admitted.

'No, you're not,' she agreed, more readily than I would have wished. 'But then, I'm no hero worshipper!'

We both laughed. Friends again. Or should I say, friends at last.

❦ ❦ ❦

Mam cried when I got home. And I said sorry for the second time that day. Then Mam and Dad said they would both forgive me, but that it wouldn't be easy. I'd have to show I was sorry as well as saying it. This process would take a while.

'It will be,' Dad said, 'in the form of instalments of sorry.'

'Sorrow,' Mam said. 'Instalments of sorrow.'

She wanted everything to be clear-cut and correct, even Dad's choice of words.

'Jobs,' Dad said. 'You'll have extra jobs, Paul. Your evenings will be fuller, from now on.'

'Mr McGrane gave me a lot of lines,' I protested feebly. I daren't say a thousand, so Dad assumed at most a hundred.

'What's a hundred lines to you? You'll rattle them off in no time. But first you'll do your jobs.'

Mam handed me a list of chores. Wash up after dinner. Make my bed. Herd the cattle. Count the sheep. Milk the polly cow. Feed the weanling calves. Draw water from the well. Bring in turf for the night. Scrub the spuds for tomorrow's dinner... I agreed meekly to this tyrannical schedule.

'Oh, and one more thing, Paul,' Mam said, almost with a smile. 'The shopping.'

'Yes, Mam, the shopping.'

'I'm changing my custom from Tommy Hodgkins. You'll have to go a bit farther in future – to Regan's new store. The food is fresher and cheaper there, anyway.'

I was glad to deprive Tommy of Mam's custom, but the extra journey far as Regan's didn't appeal to me. I muttered this truth.

'Haven't you a new bike?' Dad exclaimed. 'Courtesy of

Magpie himself. Where's the hardship in that?'

Later I could hear Mam talking in worried tones about me, after I had gone upstairs to begin my thousand lines. And I could hear Dad trying to reassure her that it was the way of all young lads nowadays to get into the odd scrape. I felt guilty as sin, and I felt resentful, too, when I thought of Raymie Boland – no doubt enjoying a good laugh at my expense. Then I heard Dad's voice again, and I stole out to the landing to listen more closely.

'I might go across,' he told Mam, 'to see Magpie one of these nights.'

'Go if you want,' she told him. 'It's a month earlier than your usual visiting time.'

'I do enjoy the chat,' he said awkwardly.

'And the game of cards,' she said. 'Don't forget that.'

'Do you mind?' he asked her. 'If you mind, I won't go.'

'I don't mind,' she told him. 'Haven't I Mrs Delaney to call on? You'd need a bit of recreation after all the hard graft.'

'I'll go, then,' Dad said. 'Just to pay my respects to Magpie. The mining company is powerful. There's a danger he mightn't be left there for long.'

7

The Apple Raid

BOLAND KEPT HIS WORD. There was no more bullying, either in the playground or on the walk from school. Whether this was due to the policeman's visit or to my efforts, I couldn't decide. I inclined towards the policeman's visit. Leastways, Boland and his gang participated in happier games. They contented themselves with hurling or chase, or with leaping games across the Darkfield River.

Other children began to join in this game. Over and back they would leap, repeatedly, and the girls were wilder than the boys. The river had steep sides, and many a time somebody would get a good dunking when they slipped and fell. Clothes would get muddied, the journey home would be cold and uncomfortable, and parents would be cross. But overall this game was good harmless fun.

My own jumping impulse would have to wait. It took four nights for me patiently to write out the thousand lines that I'd been saddled with.

Mr McGrane scanned the thick wad of foolscap:

I must never again play dangerous games on the public road.

He pursed his lips. His finger moved downward, counting off the lines. I had written them neatly but irregularly, so he couldn't easily work out how many were on each page. He had no choice but to count, and the bother of it gladdened my heart.

'...four hundred and fifty eight, four hundred and fifty nine...'

Just when he had well settled into his rhythm, Boland distracted him.

'Sir! Sir!' he yelped, jumping up out of his seat.

'Ye-e-es, Boland?' Mr McGrane said, raising one eye, but keeping his finger on the page.

'Some'un' stuck a pin in me, sir!'

'Pincushion Boland, eh? Sit down, Boland.'

'I can't, sir. Me sittin' parts is sore.'

Everybody burst into laughter at that. Mr McGrane swooped from his desk and threw Boland out the door.

'Now! Where was I?' he said, rubbing his hands as he strode back in. 'Can you tell me what number I had reached, Duggan?'

'I'm afraid not, sir. You were mumbling very low and I...'

'Very well, Duggan, don't make a Hollywood production of it.'

He would have to start once more at the beginning. I could see the pulse on the side of his face quickening, like a nervous whiplash.

One part of me felt sorry for him. Mr McGrane's problem was that he cared too much. So Cora had theorised. He wanted us all to be perfect, always to do the right thing, which you couldn't reasonably expect of children, and his wanting this so much had turned him into a class of tyrant.

Although I felt sorry for Mr McGrane, in another way I hated him for heaping misery on our unfortunate heads. Now, with the hatred and the sympathy battling, I glanced at his flustered face. It reminded me of a fiery summer sunset.

Then I made a big mistake. I winked across at Ted Connaughton. And as I did so, Mr McGrane's triumphant voice pronounced: 'Your second instalment, Duggan – a thousand more lines!'

'No,' I protested.

'You will, Duggan, and, by heavens, you'll complete a third instalment after that!'

This was more than I could stomach. Cora sympathised later, as did Ted Connaughton and several others. Raymie Boland became indignant when he heard. The fact that he had been made to stand outside the door for two hours bothered him less than my punishment. He went so far as to cancel the river game that evening, as a mark of respect, though Cora believed his real reason was that he was weary after standing all afternoon.

I told Mam. She said nothing whatsoever, but her face simmered. Dad was a talker if you vexed him, but Mam was a silence waiting to explode.

Next morning, my mother hammered on the classroom door. Mr McGrane went out to have a word with her and a heated argument seemed to erupt between them. Loud words, but few that we could actually make out. I shrank down in my desk with mortification. I thought Raymie or Pad Burns would accuse me once more of hiding behind a woman's skirts, but they were actually clenching their fists with glee and pounding them noisily on the desktops. Then Cora told Boland he was to blame for everything, and that he was a two-faced coward. Boland smashed his ruler in response, and Ted appealed for calm. Mr McGrane came meekly back in.

'Duggan, you're excused,' he said.

'Your Mam is historic,' Cora said, on the way home.

'I know she's old,' I answered, 'but I don't think she'd like being called historic.'

'I mean, she's the first person ever to complain to a teacher at Darkfield School. She's started something important.'

Cora would turn out to be right. Mam might be the first to complain, but she wouldn't be the last. Mr McGrane's power was beginning to wane.

❦ ❦ ❦

I began to join in the river-jumping game. There was an energy in me that wouldn't die down. I became a bigger devil than most. Raymie Boland must have seen this as a sign that he could involve me again in his schemes. He grew all conversational. I found it hard to be shut of him, yapping constantly at my shoulder. He told me about his pet guinea fowl and about how to set snares for rabbits and about the time his mam had killed a pig to provide meat for the family because his dad was too delicate to do it. Yes, 'delicate' was the word he used, but even I knew his dad better than that.

'I'm come into some money,' he said, one evening.

'Has the mining company paid your Dad for his farm, or what?'

'No. He got a lend off'a' the bank, on the strength of it, see.'

We went into Tommy's shop, but immediately the ginger eyebrows bristled, the finger pointed.

'I'll serve you, Boland, but not that scamp.' Tommy wasn't about to forget the road-snoozing incident in a hurry.

Raymie bought a whole can of clove sweets, and we munched them on the way home. I thought for a moment of the broken front tooth he'd given me months before, and as if reading my mind he said: 'It improves ya, that gap in the gob.' Then he laughed – a friendly laugh – and what could I do but laugh with him?

'We're movin' tonight,' he said then.

'Your family?' I asked, half-hoping.

'Ah, don't be a gobdaw, Paul! It don't suit ya. No, I'm talkin' 'bout me an' the lads. We have a mark set.'

'A target? Who?' He had my undivided attention now.

'That oul' cod they call the Magpie, beyond.'

His words knocked the wind out of me better than a punch in the stomach could.

'Why him?' I managed to ask. 'What have ye in mind?'

'Eatin' apples, what else?' Boland said, those teeth of his gnawing again as if anticipating the fresh clean bite. 'Magpie has powerful apples, the best in the parish. We'll use five canvas bags, that'd be 'bout enough to clean 'im out. He deserves it fer tryin' to stop the mine. He's cracked as a bottle, that lad. Come in wi' us. We'll share 'em bags, one bag apiece.'

Robbing orchards was a favourite occupation of ours in Darkfield. Conscience didn't come into it, usually. But the idea of robbing Magpie's apples was something I would never go with. And I had learned my lesson, as far as Raymie's ploys and schemes were concerned. I would run a mile. But I decided to play along for a while, just to gain more information.

'When are you doing it?' I asked. 'There's no great hurry, is there? Can't you take your time, plan it properly?'

'Good on ya, Paul, ever the brains! An' I have it fixed already. Tonight's a full moon. We'll need to see what we're at. Anyways, we can't wait. The oul' cod might be pickin' them apples himsel' any day now, then we could scratch. An' you know, Paul, we could sell them apples at the Ballinasloe Fair. We made ten quid last year on oul' John Hobbins' crab apples. Thass chickenfeed compared to Magpie's. They'd be worth thirty quid, easy. Enough to keep us flush fer the winter.'

Raymie had it all fixed, just as he'd said. Nine o'clock was the time he'd set for the raid to take place. Magpie could whistle, after that. I decided to try one more stalling tactic.

'You don't need the money, Raymie, do you? Not with the mine buying up your Dad's farm and all?'

'The oul' fella's pockets might be deep, thass true. 'Ceptin' he'll be on the jar constant, like. He'd turn barley grains into booze if'n he could! An' he'd deprive ya of the very daylight, them times. But ya see, the money's only part of it. The highs is what I'm after. A piece of sport, if'n nothin' else.'

I was silently cursing the whole misfortune that was Raymie Boland. And I regretted the delay in getting home. For it was almost teatime. The river-leaping and the sweet-eating had kept us until now. I'd be too late to warn Magpie. It wasn't as if I could phone him or anything. He had no phone. And darkness had already begun to fall.

'But Raymie…' I began.

'But nothin!'' Raymie said. 'Yer in with us, aren't ya? You've earned the right, Paul. Ya never ratted on me to McGrane. Fact, ya damn near broke 'im wi' yer willpower!'

'Why didn't you give me enough notice?' I asked, pretending to be annoyed. 'I can't go tonight! My family's going down to Aunt Florence's in Athlone. There's no way they would let me stay on my own in the house.'

'Ah, sorry Paul. I should'a give ya more notice. Next time, ha?'

'Next time,' I echoed. 'And make sure to keep a few apples for me, won't you?'

Now, I know what you're thinking. You're thinking I should cut my losses and tell my dad, and let him warn Magpie. And I would have, if that were possible. But I had only partly lied to Raymie about the family not being at home. Dad, in fact, *wasn't* at home. He had chosen that evening to visit his sister, my demented Aunt Florence.

Aunt Florence was forever calling him away to mend a gatepost or a fence or whatnot. She had after all to cope on her own, Mam gave me to understand. And she was overly refined, and worried thin with bad health. Dad wouldn't be back until God alone knew when. And Mam wouldn't let me across at that hour of the evening, with the Callows flooded and the darkness down early now.

But I'd have to go across, regardless. I had to warn Magpie of the impending raid.

I couldn't eat much dinner. Sick with worry and sick with sweets. Mam was in an unforgiving humour.

'This day of all days,' she said, 'you might have got home sooner, knowing your Dad would be away. Well, my fine son, the jobs are all to do, and you'll do them, what's more. I wouldn't mind but I even told your Dad to buy that Valour comic for you while he's out! More fool me, I suppose.'

I set about my stack of chores. Counted, herded, milked, fed and gathered, reflecting that Captain Valour never had to concern himself with such menial tasks. All he had to bother him was the business of saving the world. Magpie O'Brien was the real Valour, it seemed, limited and fragile though he might be, preyed on by Darkfield Mining Enterprises, with the insult of Raymie Boland added on for a final twist. I hurried here and there about my work, and the noise of the mine provided a backdrop to my unsettled thoughts.

Yes, quietness had become a thing of the past in Darkfield. Grind and clang and thrum had started out of the blue, early one morning, and never since stopped. They were building and ripping and pushing things aside, there at the far end of the Callows, and the din rolled across to us, day and night. How much worse must it be for Magpie, living close to the mine, I wondered. The voice of the corncrake, which he had pretended to complain about, would be sheer bliss compared to the mining racket. Now the corncrake had flown, and the cuckoo too, and the grey geese would land soon, but the noise of the machines would drown out their laughter.

My last chore for the night was to take the bed linen in from the washing line. Mam's mood wasn't improved when she saw it. Her precious white sheets were covered with a fine dust, which left them looking soiled and old.

'Did you drag them through the muck?' she asked.

'No, I folded them. They never touched the ground,' I assured her.

Then we understood what had happened. Dust from the mine had been borne over on the wind, lightly coating pathways, windowpanes, grass – and Mam's sheets. This misfortune was destined to happen several times in the future. Mam couldn't be pacified. She took out her temper on the washing board, scrubbing those sheets for dear life.

❦ ❦ ❦

The kitchen clock said quarter past eight. I'd need to move soon if I was to warn Magpie. I made my excuses and headed straight for my bedroom.

'No wonder you're tired,' she called after me. 'You spend more time gallivanting than a lad your age should.'

If only she knew the truth, she'd skin me alive. And then a softer note came into her voice. 'In future could you please come home just a little bit earlier for your dinner?'

'Yes, Mam,' I sighed, taking to the stairs with a trudge in my feet. 'Goodnight!'

'Goodnight, child.'

My bedroom window opened onto the flat-roofed back porch. Sometimes I'd sit out there for a while, before hitting the mattress. There was always the hope that Will o' the Wisp might appear. Lately I had noticed not his light, but instead the lights of the mine, beginning to bloom. Steady, distant, twinkling with a stern energy, they seemed to augment the mine noise. There weren't many of them yet, but soon there would be a sprawl. Soon I would have a lit-up horizon to gaze out at. Then the spirit of the Callows might rise and do his ghostly, gallivanting dance, but I would never be able to see him.

That night I stood at the window fretting. The big harvest moon cast a silvery light over everything. I opened the window and stepped out. The porch had an indented series of lines sunk into its walls for decorative effect, and these were nearly as good as ladder-rungs to me. I let myself down carefully, silently, leaving Mam none the wiser. I stole round to Dad's utility shed and found my wellingtons and a flashlamp. Then I set off across the Callows.

I might have been lost, if not drowned, but for the moon. I thought of what Magpie had said about an intervention of the heavens saving him from Keaveney's Quag when he was young. Then again, if it were not for the moon, there might have been no apple raid, and consequently no need for this journey.

I kept to the higher ground, sloshed through the safer loughs. Once, I was startled by a hissing noise, and my flashlamp shone on the craning necks and yellow throats of five vivid-white swans. Mostly, though, there was the dull drone of the mine, and the gleam of the mine lights, pointing me in their direction.

When I came within sight of Magpie's gate, I switched off the flashlamp. I crept closer and was about to climb the gate when I heard a rustle in the orchard within. My heart skipped a beat. The robbery had already begun.

I stood stock-still, listened. There was the scrunch of a foot on a fallen apple, then a whispered curse. Raymie reprimanding Pad. I crouched low, wondering what I should do. I didn't dare climb the gate – it would rattle. Besides, climbing would make me too visible.

Where was Magpie? Had he gone to bed early? I could see no flicker of candlelight in his little window. And where was Riff-raff? Not where I wanted him to be, that's for sure! I squatted there, hoping he would sneak up on Raymie's gang, and do a bit of damage. Maybe even alert Magpie. No sign of him, though.

I crawled on all fours along by the privet hedge that threw its protective arm around Magpie's orchard. The cold, wet earth shocked my knees. I peered through a low gap in the hedge. Shadows moved carefully about, criss-crossed, stopped. The ground was bare under the crooked trees. I lifted my head. The prize apples were visible to me, silver-yellow in the moonlight, hung amid crisp leaves that had begun to wither.

Then I saw Raymie's face. He turned his head around until he seemed to be gaping right at me. But no, he was talking to Dervan, whose back was facing towards the hedge, almost within touching distance now.

'That blackguard Magpie's after pickin' half of 'em!' Boland hissed. 'There don't seem to be as many as I saw a bare month ago.'

'Have you been casin' the place for that length?' Dervan asked.

''Course I have!' Raymie answered. 'How else would I know about 'im sendin' that peculiar dog of his to bed in the evenin's?' Then he laughed, quietly. 'Thass why I get extra apples – fer the extra work I been puttin' in.'

There were no disagreements from the others. Raymie pointed them to their allotted trees. I saw Pad and Dervan fan out, each with a large canvas bag in tow, but I didn't see Hynes at all. Raymie had chosen for himself the four trees whose branches over-leaned the galvanise-roofed shed. He tossed two canvas bags up, then I saw him climb onto the shed in one fluent lift of his sturdy arms. He danced confidently to the front portion of the roof, believing, no doubt, that the noise from the mine would leave him unheard.

I scanned among the trees for a sighting of Hynes, to no avail. The branches of each tree made a cup-shape. Magpie had told me once that this was the correct way to prune apple trees, so they would catch plenty of light. Sure enough, only the undersides of the branches wore dark smudges, where the moon failed to reach. The same would presumably apply where sunshine was concerned. But I wasn't thinking of that now. I put the mystery of Hynes' whereabouts aside, and resumed my crawl.

The privet hedge brought me around to a gate next the farther gable of Magpie's house. I could see Raymie clearly from there, and follow the sway of branches where he reached. I waited for a suitable moment, and finally it came. Raymie let an apple fall, and stooped to retrieve it. Immediately I stood up. I stepped onto the first rung of the gate. It made no rattle. I was about to step onto the second rung when a hand clamped hard across my mouth, and another pinioned me by the arms.

Hynes had been on lookout, of course. He had tracked me to the gate, then pounced. He dragged me backwards a distance, forced me through a weak spot in the hedge, and into the orchard. All my scuffling struggles couldn't rescue the situation. Boland saw what was happening, for he immediately jumped from the shed. Then he, Pad Burns and Dervan nailed me as I tried to regain my feet.

Boland wrestled off my coat and tore my shirt in strips. Some of the strips he used as a gag for my mouth, and he tied my arms and legs together behind my back with the remainder. I was frantic, caught in a slow, helpless struggle, but they carried relentlessly on. Eventually, they shunted me head-first into the shed. I heard the iron bolt slip back into place behind me.

I lay helpless in the dark musty shed. I wrenched my wrists for all I was worth, trying to lever them free, but nobody could tie a knot the way Raymie Boland could. He was expert in that, the hog-tier supreme. The gag he'd fastened chafed my mouth. The metallic taste of blood came to my tongue. I could do nothing but lie sideways against the shed wall, heaving breaths through my nostrils.

Outside, they had begun again. I heard the slight creak of galvanise, the steps that must be Raymie's, moving about gently above my head. Only once was there the thump and roll of an apple escaping his clutch. A few times I heard the dragged weight of the bags he was filling, as he adjusted them to suit the tree he was picking from, then a final thud when he and his apple-hoard came down.

I was left behind in the dark, musty concrete shed, and my humiliation burned. I had failed my friend, Magpie. No amount of useless tears could alter that fact. I blinked my eyes. Then I became aware of a window in the wall facing me, a small window with four panes of glass. Maybe I could escape through it? Immediately the notion died. I was tied in such a way that I couldn't walk, let alone climb. There would be no chance to warn Magpie, to claim his apples back. I dragged myself towards the window. It allowed in the faint moonlight.

Just then I became aware of another presence in the shed. As my heart missed a beat I realised it was a dog presence, emerging from the blackest corner. It was Riff-raff, and as I moved, so he moved towards me. I saw his teeth bare themselves a moment, and felt afraid. Then he reached his muzzle in to sniff my face. I was helpless but he didn't bite. He simply lay down quite near, and stared at me for a long while, and let his head lean onto his paws.

I snuffled at him through my gagging cloth. I rolled towards him, trying to kick. I was desperate to make him bark, so Magpie might come and investigate. He remained mute. The only dog I had ever met that wouldn't bark, whatever the situation. Riff-raff lay beside me in the dark shed all that long desperate night, until finally, exhausted and in pain, I must have fallen asleep.

8

Rescued

ONE MOMENT I WAS ASLEEP, and what seemed like the next, I had snapped my eyes open. Two big wrinkled hands were turning me around. It was Magpie, all concern, leaning over me. His cold knuckles touched my forehead gently.

'Ah child, is it yourself?' he said, his voice strange.

He undid my binds. I shivered into his bony embrace, sobbing out the whole sorry story, desperate to explain.

'Don't I know,' he kept saying. 'Don't I know well.'

Then he placed my coat over my bare shoulders.

'Turn around, Paul,' he said, after a few moments. 'Riff--raff wants to talk to you.'

'He can't talk,' I said. 'He can't even bark.'

Riff-raff came close to my face, touched it with his cold muzzle, stared at me softly.

'He'd talk if he could,' Magpie said. 'I was telling you a fable previously about him not botherin' to bark, being near his kinfolk, the foxes. The real reason he don't bark is because he has no tongue. He lost it in a trap some casual farmer set for rats. That's the why he don't talk. That's how he's prone to nip people. He wants to lick 'em, to make a communication, but he ain't got the tongue.'

'He didn't nip me,' I told Magpie.

'Ain't that because there's already a communication established between?' the old man said. 'He took to you. You took to him.'

I patted Riff-raff's head with both my hands. I felt sad for him as much as for myself. His cold, wet nose was balm to my hot, chafed wrists.

'I couldn't save your orchard,' I said. 'Everything's ruined.'

'No, it ain't,' he said brightly. 'Look up there, at them rafters.'

My gaze followed Magpie's wonder-rounded eyes. I could scarcely believe what I saw above us.

Four roughly cylindrical shapes hung from silken threads attached to the rafters. They were pulsing gently. Alive!

'Pupae,' Magpie said. 'Butterfly pupae, if I'm not mistaken. Fruit of the orchard out yonder. There's some would call them chrysalides.'

Whatever they might be called, they were not like anything I'd ever seen. These were larger than pupae had a right to be.

'They're enormous,' I gasped.

'They are, right enough. Each must be nearly big as your two hands.'

I joined my hands before me. That was just about the size and shape each pupa made.

'Four prayers,' Magpie said quietly. 'Four prayers for the world. And yours the fifth.'

He pointed out the impression of wings on each pupa case, the spike-covered head and thorax region, and the series of bumps and ring-marks where the legs and abdomen would form.

'They been my secret this past while,' he said. 'I discerned them when they were caterpillars. Huge, hairy caterpillars! You'd think they might have a taste for leaves of cabbage, or nettles even, the way some caterpillars do. Not a chance! They were partial to my apples, of course, and I let them take what they required.'

Then he chuckled softly and ran a big, gnarled hand through his black-and-white streaked hair. 'There couldn't be a whole pile left for them bucks who came to rob me,' he said.

I had all but forgotten my grievances. I sat fascinated by the sight above us and by what Magpie was saying, and Riff-raff sat next to me.

'They got sleepy, you know,' Magpie continued. 'They got plump and sleepy. Then one evening I espied them in here, hanging on silk ropes, their mouths weaving away.'

'Why are they here?' I asked. 'What does it mean, them being here?'

'I don't know where they come from,' he answered. 'Maybe they're an exotic species, borne over by chance from the sub-continent of India, or the Rondonian Rainforest, or some such mitred place. I haven't a clue where they come from, and I'm not bothered.'

His hands gripped my shoulders, and his face trembled with emotion. 'Will you mind them with me, Paul? Our secret, and ours alone? Until the springtime sees them emerge? Will you now?'

I swore that I would. And as the dawn sun broke in through the small window, it revealed to us tiny rivulets of blood flowing sluggishly inside each pupa. Then Magpie raised me above his head to touch one – the effort made him dizzy – and the pupa twitched slightly under my fingertips. I felt the wonder of the world beating inside my mind. We turned and made our way out into the broad daylight.

'Do you hear it?' Magpie said then, jerking his head in the direction of the mine. 'It's drawing closer by the day, that cursed pit. Soon it'll be forenenst me.'

'Will you bring me over to see it?' I asked.

'Some other time,' he said. 'Your parents might be worrying about you just now.'

So Magpie accompanied me homeward, with Riff-raff bounding ahead of us through the Callows.

When you have someone to champion you, you can face any hardship. And I know it's a terrible thing to say, but just then, the thought of facing my parents seemed like a hardship. I was glad Magpie was with me.

'I'll clarify it all in plain language,' he assured me. 'And in the meanwhile, we might find the stroll a suitable distraction.'

He insisted we follow the same sidewise and backward paths that we had taken during our previous crossing. A courtesy to the Callows, he called it. We came to the drainage ditches, and negotiated each narrow bridge. And where there was no bridge I helped him drag somehow through to the other side.

'Marl,' he said at one point, stumbling and coming up with a handful of creamy white clay. 'It lies under the entire Callows, Paul.'

Slowly he rubbed the marl between his palms, extracting from it what appeared to be little grainy stones. These he washed clean in the drain itself, before placing them into my hand.

'Snail shells!' I exclaimed. 'How can that be?'

'Where you're standing now, and roun' about everywhere here,' he said with a smile, 'was all a lake, oh thousands and thousands of years ago.'

Magpie was right. The Callows had their distracting wonders and I temporarily forgot my worries. Finally we drew near to home. Mam and Dad were eating breakfast. I could smell the Saturday fry as we reached the porch door. Naturally we didn't knock. And there sat the pan on the range, with my helping of sausages and rashers sizzling quietly. No doubt Mam and Dad were expecting me to come thumping down the stairs at any minute. Probably had been shouting for ages that I should come down. Their mouths fell open when we walked in on top of them. Riff-raff, at least, stayed outside. They were shocked, I suppose, at the state of me, but Magpie immediately set about soothing their fret.

'I'll take up your cause,' Dad shouted. 'I'll take up your cause with that Raymie Boland's father.'

Dad rose from the table with his fists closed by his sides, and his face set in a grimace. He danced about the kitchen. He issued a stream of warry talk. Magpie just sat calmly watching and nodding, making sympathetic noises until the show of temper cooled.

Mam gave my breakfast to Magpie. He took it, what's more. She then went upstairs, stepping quietly. There she ran a hot-water tub for me. I waited until she came back down before going up. I knew she would say nothing against me with Magpie present. You could read Mam easily as a book. She had fierce pride. After I had bathed, she doctored me over with plasters as only she could.

'You've had plenty of practice, Mam,' I said, forgetting to be tactful.

She didn't appreciate the joke. In fact her answer was to take from the dresser the latest issue of Captain Valour, which Dad had just bought, and to shred it page by page, right before my eyes.

❦ ❦ ❦

I skipped some days from school, and when I returned, there stood Pad Burns, and Dervan in the yard, slouching and grinning stupidly and kicking at imaginary objects while we waited for the bell. I could look each of them in the eye, but they seemed unable to answer my stare.

'Where's Raymie Boland?' I asked Cora.

'He's been absent for the same length of time as you have,' she said. 'I thought you might have seen him.'

When I told her about the apple raid, she threw her eyes up to heaven in exasperation.

'You're hopeless, Paul,' she sighed. 'There have always been apple raids in Darkfield, and you still try to stop one, even to the point of getting mixed up with Boland again. You deserved to be locked in Magpie's shed!'

That was that. I wouldn't be telling Cora the rest of the story – about the gigantic pupae – in a hurry. Or maybe, I would tell her part of it, as a tease...

Mr McGrane spent the morning talking about the electric and magnetic properties of rocks. No doubt he felt we ought to understand such things, since we'd be living with Darkfield Mining Enterprises in our midst for the foreseeable future. I raised my hand. I wanted to tell him about the constant grinding noise, and the fine dust that had fallen on Mam's sheets. I wanted especially to advertise Magpie's protest group, AMID. He waved my hand down.

'Most rocks are plain dead,' he explained. 'But metallic rocks are full of energy. They're the life and soul of the party, by comparison. Geologists can measure the difference.'

He took a long tube of rock from his desk and held it up.

'This comes from far underground,' he explained. 'It's called core rock. The geologists drilled many samples of core rock. They made a map of the metallic rocks under the clays of Darkfield. They must have liked the jizz and energy of this rock, because now they've started the mine.'

He passed the tube of rock to the front desk. Eventually it made its way down to where Cora and I sat. It was perfectly smooth, with white streaks running alongside its dark tones. At top and bottom, where it had been broken off from a longer segment, there were several glinting pieces. Cora put up her hand.

'Are these bits of silver?' she asked, pointing.

'No, indeed,' Mr McGrane said. 'They're called mica. They have no value whatsoever.'

Everyone was allowed to talk about the rock for a while. A mumble rose around the classroom.

'Mr McGrane is good when he sticks to teaching,' I told Cora, trying to get back on friendly terms. 'I mean, when he leaves our lives outside the classroom to mind themselves.'

'If only you could mind your life outside the classroom,' she said waspishly.

'I have a new power word,' I said, annoyed.

'Tell us then.'

'Pupae.'

'You mean butterfly pupae? That doesn't sound much. Where's the power in pupae?'

'It's an amazingly powerful power word,' I assured her. 'The most powerful power word in the whole world.'

'What does it do? Turn you into a sissy?'

'No use being sarcastic,' I said. 'Or you'll never learn the secret.'

That evening, and each evening afterward, I came home

promptly – for Mam's sake more than my own. The strained look gradually left her face. She praised me for being sensible. 'Sensible despite the strange times we're living in,' she said, referring to Darkfield Mine and the changes that were afoot.

More strangers came. Their accents and their clothes were different from ours. Denim and corduroy began to be favoured by the youth of Darkfield. Leather was out of reach still, being too expensive. But some teenagers bought records and threw arrogant shapes, and drank and smoked.

It would probably have happened anyway, but it happened quicker due to the presence of the strangers. These men went about the place as if they owned it. They probably did own it, or at least they worked for the men who owned it, and to confuse things further, there was that name, *Darkfield Mining Enterprises Limited.* They put up this biggest of all signs at the broad entrance to the mine where – it was reported – giant gates made of gold would soon be erected.

❦ ❦ ❦

So much happens beyond eye-level when you're aged eleven-and-three-quarters, trying to fix your place in the world. And so much more passes straight over your head. You go around in a kind of daze. Leastways, I did. Magpie's campaign had moved on without me. Dad attended meetings, but insisted I was too young to go. He visited Magpie's house some nights.

'How's Magpie? What does he say?' I'd question him afterwards.

'He understands you're constrained by school.'

I began to feel guilty regardless, at not supporting Magpie. Then Dad took to writing letters against open-cast mining, and he gave me the job of correcting his spellings and toning down the odd extravagant word. I was delighted to help, especially since he told me that he showed all the letters to Magpie before sending them off for publication. There was a peculiar thrill in seeing Dad's name at the foot of the letters, whether they appeared in local or national newspapers, and in running a finger over the exact phrases that I had helped him to select.

I felt removed from the real centre of action, however. The thrumming mine-noise seemed to tease me with its every change of gear. The tube of core rock, which had felt so heavy and so strange in my hand, and which now held pride of place on our classroom nature table, made me wish to see exactly what was going on at the mine site. I decided to follow the machines – via my usual route through the Callows.

'I'll go with you,' Dad declared. 'I have to admit that I pride myself on my technical knowledge. I might be able to communicate some of it to you, and then you can amaze Mr McGrane at school.'

No doubt Mr McGrane had already been sufficiently amazed, but I stayed quiet, not wanting to spoil Dad's innocence. Normally I'd be delighted to walk across with him, but now it just meant that I wouldn't be able to look in on the butterfly pupae in Magpie's shed.

'I have a favour to ask of that lad,' Dad said cryptically, as we neared Magpie's house. 'I'm sure he won't refuse me.'

Wouldn't you know it, the favour had to do with letting me see the pupae! I couldn't believe Magpie had told Dad. I sulked a bit, to tell you the God's honest.

'Our secret, and ours alone.' Weren't these Magpie's

exact words, after all? But, of course, I forgave him.

And the four pupae hung from the rafters in splendour still, their speckled and spiked grey-green cases enfolding a promise we could only guess at.

'I'll give ye the guided tour,' Magpie said, after we had emerged into the haggard again. There was a sprinkling of black dust over the cobblestones. We unlocked the gate where Hynes had nabbed me, and headed for the mine. Magpie drew some cotton wool from his pocket and gave us a wodge of it each, to counteract the noise.

'It must be an affliction, living so close,' Dad commented.

'It is,' Magpie agreed. 'But ain't I a buffer zone between, just the same?'

Then he complimented me on the letters I'd been helping Dad to write to the newspapers. 'Polished' was the word he used to describe them.

'What the use of letters?' I asked. 'The mine is happening anyway.'

'The letters have started a debate,' he told me. 'There's others now, from all over Ireland, talking about that mine. And there's many in agreement with our stance.'

Still, when we reached the mine-lands, I think even Dad was shocked at what we saw. The topsoil had been stripped off and pushed in over a vast tract of bogland, which lay on the far side of the mine. Trees, hedges, grasses, all were gone. The complete absence of greenness appalled us. But there was a large blue lake, which I certainly didn't remember seeing previously, held between low concrete walls.

'That used to be a harmless stream,' Magpie said sorrowfully. 'They've circumvented it to make a tailings pond. They'll be washing their poison there soon.'

He and Dad recognised some local men who were operating the excavators and driving the trucks and constructing the buildings. The men shouted and waved. Dad named the machines for me. These included face shovels, loaders, dumpers, and bulldozers. Cement mixers I had seen before, but never so many in one location. Their grey abdomens gargled noisily as they fed the scaffolded sites. Dad spoke monotonously. Technical expert he might call himself, but his heart wasn't in it.

'All that clay,' I said. 'All those fields and trees. Gone.'

'Overburden,' Magpie said. 'That's the name the mining company use. They want to get at the minerals underneath.'

'How far down?' I asked.

'Not far,' Dad answered. 'About as deep as our back porch, if you were to bury it.'

Dad had a way of making things simple and vivid. And I had a way of complicating them on him again. 'How many times would our porch fit into the overburden?' I asked.

He scratched his head, scanned far and wide about him. 'A million times,' he said.

A million parcels of clay, each the size of our porch. *Big* was a small word when you used it to describe how the mine would be. And when something that big comes into existence, other things have to disappear just to make room for it. Not just grasses and hedges and cows and trees, but houses and people as well.

Families who had always been our neighbours, began to pack their belongings and move away. It was all quick and casual. You might hear news of their departure a day or two before they left. Or a day or two afterwards. You'd say to yourself: 'Well, I'm used to this now. I'll know to expect it in future. I'll not be caught on the hop any more.' But when the next family left, you'd be surprised all over again. And you'd feel poor, somehow. There'd be a gap, as if those people who had left the village had also left an empty space where they had specially existed, inside your mind and inside your heart.

9

The Coming of Spring

THAT WINTER WAS ONE OF THE WETTEST in living memory. The Callows flooded over. I didn't get to see Magpie or the pupae as often as I would have liked. I felt sorry for him, 'holding out against progress', as even the more reasonable people in Darkfield inclined to believe.

The Christmas holidays came and went. Cora Delaney actually gave me a fountain pen as a gift. I was startled that she should think of doing this. After all, we'd had our fair share of squabbles and besides, I wouldn't have dreamt of buying her a present.

'Open it,' she said.

'A golden nib. *Very* nice, Cora,' I said, awkwardly.

'No. Open the fountain pen is what I mean.'

I unscrewed its middle. Inside was a long black rubber tube, which would contain the ink.

'It's ... primitive,' I said.

'The exact word!' Cora agreed. 'It's primitive as the devil's coach-horse you keep for a pet under that big stone. It even looks like him.'

'I haven't seen that fellow in ages,' I told her. 'I wonder if he's still alive.'

We both went to check. The pet insect was nowhere to

be found when I tilted the boundary stone. Only a mean-looking centipede – which reminded me of one of Tommy Hodgkins' eyebrows – scurried into the grass. And a cluster of woodlice slowly unsettled itself. I felt sad at having ignored the devil's coach-horse. Just as I had ignored Captain Valour, refusing even to sneak a look at him in Kelly's shop window, whenever Mam brought me to town.

'Issue 102 must be out by now,' Mam would say, wanting to compensate for having destroyed Issue 101, but somehow I had outgrown the Captain. I couldn't take his bombastic deeds and his high-falutin' words seriously any more.

The pet insect was a different matter, however. I had let our relationship lapse, and now he was probably dead. I said all this to Cora.

'At least you still have 'pupae', your mysterious power word,' she replied.

'That's true,' I agreed. 'And I'm waiting for it to incubate.'

'You're waiting for the pupae to incubate,' she repeated, trying to make sense of it.

I could tell she was bursting with curiosity, but she didn't ask me to reveal the secret. Then the notion struck me that I would tell her anyway. I'd tell her simply because she hadn't asked. Besides, Magpie had told Dad. Why shouldn't I tell Cora? So I did – on condition that she would cross the Callows with me when the time came for the pupae to emerge – and she was suitably astounded.

❦ ❦ ❦

A few weeks later the floods eased, and I visited Magpie. I was shocked to see him wearing an old gas mask – from the

First World War, he said. It was a tactic against the mine dust. He looked a holy terror, I can tell you, in that green gas mask that was hard and tinny and had a long, griddled muzzle. But I didn't laugh. I simply feared that he might be losing his mind. Again he gave me cotton wool for my ears.

'I ain't able to hear them crickets any more,' he complained. 'But come with me, Paul. I'll draw a drop of water so we can wet the tea.' Out I went with him to the well.

Magpie's well looked different from any other well I had ever laid eyes on. It was contained within a walled tunnel going deep, deep into the earth. I didn't think at all of it as a water-dragon's tail – so much for dad's overactive imagination! And the well was actually covered with a heavy blanket – to keep the dust off, as Magpie reminded me. We both had to take enormous care whilst removing the blanket.

'Boring this well was the first and last time gelignite was used in Darkfield,' Magpie told me. 'Until now.'

I dropped a pebble towards the perfect silver circle of water far below. Some seconds later, we heard the plop. Magpie wasn't pleased.

'That might have been a pollutant,' he said. 'If it ain't poisoned my supply, I'll be lucky.'

'It's just a stone,' I said, hurt by his words.

'Stones ain't what they used to be,' he countered.

He had grown edgy, yet how could I fault him? He was at war, after all. But he could still move nimbly on his toes. He fastened a long rope to his bucket and dropped the bucket in. Dunk! One leg danced across the well's opening so that he kind of straddled it. A dangerous manoeuvre, but I said nothing. He must know what he was doing. He'd been doing it for more than eighty years. I was happy just to watch his wrists working the rope. They put me in mind of the way Dad's hands moved, tackling Jack the pony.

I carried the water back to the house, and Magpie brewed tea. I sipped, he slurped, the noise of machinery filtered through our makeshift cotton-wool earmuffs. Riff-raff came and sat by my ruptured armchair. He rested his chin on my wellington boot. The wet log in the fire smoked and sizzled, then launched a spangle of vicious sparks onto the hearthstone. Riff-raff jumped.

I didn't tell Magpie that Cora now knew the secret of the orchard. Nor did I mention the absence of my devil's coach-horse. I didn't want to depress him any further. He stood up slowly, and took a hard-covered book from the top of the dresser, and left it onto my lap. Inside were sketches of Callows flowers and birds, and carefully penned reminiscences about the Callows themselves.

'Keep this, won't you?' he said. 'It contains my happiest days. The idle days I spent looking.'

I knew well enough not to argue. I placed the book under my arm, and promised that I would keep it safely, and return it in good time. He chuckled softly, then we went to see the mine.

The wet weather had done nothing to stop the work. The topsoil had been completely cleared, and the plant was all in place. I told Magpie I thought 'plant' was a strange word for man-made things.

'It's a word,' Magpie explained, 'by which they mean buildings, conveyor belts, machines.'

And what buildings! A huge one called the Crusher, sunk in the side of a mound. There the loads of ore-rock were being dumped and broken down, before being conveyed on to the second giant building, the Concentrator Mill.

'That's the biggest building ever raised in the west of

Ireland,' Magpie told me. 'And one of the fastest to be built, if I ain't mistaken. It's strange how quickly people can operate, at the prospect of money. They'd work day and night, Saturday and Sunday. Bless 'em, despite.'

'What's happening inside the Mill?' I asked.

'That's where the different ores – lead, zinc, cadmium and others – are being separated from the unvalued stuff.'

He turned to face me. 'Ah, but I have no fault with them mining men,' he said. 'They are a decent enough crowd. They give me lifts into town so I can collect my pension.'

He fumbled in his breast pocket and removed a few nuggets of rock, with little mica moons shining in them. These he gave to me, and began to dig inside his pocket for more. Meanwhile I was watching the excavators at work, tearing out the ore-bearing rocks. Heavy-wheeled trucks wove through the black mire, down to the open pits. They skidded and slid and left criss-crossed snake-patterns of tyres behind them. I became fascinated, watching from that hillock at the edge of Magpie's land. I didn't think beyond the moment. I didn't think of the fact that I was standing on the one spot which Darkfield Mining Enterprises still hadn't got their clutches on. The one spot they wanted most of all.

Suddenly, Magpie dropped a heavy shard of rock into my hand, and I got a fright. It was a rough, black stone, with maybe a million pinheads of light glimmering, to no great effect, on its surface.

'Dull, ain't it?' he said. 'Dull, though it contains real silver.'

We were silent a while. Him and me, and the precious book tucked under my arm.

'It would turn any youngster's head, that mine,' he said then. 'It's a fever that drives grown men the world over, so why not a boy? I don't blame you, lad.'

'They promise to landscape it when they're done,' I told him. 'They'll push the soil back into place, and it will grow trees and grass again.'

He chuckled, then placed his hand on my shoulder. 'Ah Paul, I wish I could believe them,' he said sadly. 'And maybe they do mean to landscape it all. Maybe they're genuine, after a fashion.'

He pointed over at the huge damned lake that had been created, some distance from us. It looked white-grey now, not blue.

'Fifty decent fields lie under that tailings pond,' he said. 'Nothing will ever grow in or around or under that pond again. And nothing will fly over it, 'cept maybe a plane.'

I felt heart-broken at Magpie's words.

'Will the Callows be safe?' I asked. 'Will we be able to protect the orchard?'

'That's the why I'm saying 'No' to them besuited gentlemen. Long as I say 'No', the Callows will live. Them Callows couldn't bear being any closer to the mine than they are. They'll perish if the mine moves any closer to them.'

We returned with heavy hearts to his haggard. Spring had come unnoticed by us until now. Daffodils grew in tufts near his gable. Golden daffodils, yes, but when I touched them, a black coating of dust came away on my fingers. I tasted it. Metallic, but not of blood. More metallic than the dust that had fallen on Mam's and Dad's farm, on our own slate-roofed house.

'We have one more call to make,' Magpie said.

We went into the galvanised shed to see the pupae. They seemed ripe, pulsing steadily within themselves, though they hung perfectly still.

'Soon the emergence will happen,' Magpie decided.

This thought, and a glimpse of newly sprouted leaves in the orchard, filled me with renewed hope.

❦ ❦ ❦

I showed the shard of silver to Mam and Dad when I arrived home. It was dull, just as Magpie had said, but it nonetheless possessed a certain twinkle. And when touched by sunlight or lamplight, it glittered all the more. I decided to glue it onto my bedroom wall to catch the movement of Will o' the Wisp, to alert me when he was dancing the Callows. Dad said I was probably wasting my time. The lights of Darkfield Mine would soon outshine that pale spirit.

I didn't blame the miners for what was happening. They just wanted to earn a living for themselves and their families. And the job they did was hard. Hard and dangerous.

Lorries passed the road every few minutes, taking the ore away from us, away to Galway Port, from where it would be shipped to the far-flung world. Fifty lorries made that journey, each day. And each lorry did so four times.

I calculated it all for Mr McGrane. That amount of travel was the same as two hundred lorry loads of ore being moved from Darkfield each day. Already there was talk of the road being widened, and the city port being deepened. The sleepy local towns had begun to boom.

I put up my hand. I would tell the teacher about the convoy of lorries and the fact that he needn't worry his head – none of us would be road-snoozing again.

❦ ❦ ❦

There was no sign of Raymie Boland appearing back at school, though we were now deep into spring. He had often taken days off on account of hating Mr McGrane, or on account of his dad being on the drink. Whichever – it was a toss up. But he had never been absent for so many days.

'Count your blessings,' Cora said. 'You're actually quite normal when he's not around.'

She spoke the truth. I avoided Pad Burns and his gang. Yes, he had become the leader, in Raymie's absence. But it was a toothless gang, with a brainless leader. It did nothing but make stupid dares. Who can spit the farthest? Who can wade through Darkfield River in his bare feet? Who can rob the magpie eggs on top of old John Hobbins' wood?

'I'm only mindin' things till Raymie comes back,' Pad assured me, as if I cared.

'You're doing a mighty job, Pad,' I replied. 'You should take over altogether.'

'Ah now, don't be saying that in case Raymie gets wind of it,' he answered, caught between pride and nervousness.

Then one evening as Cora and I were making our way from school, a big truck pulled up in front of us, and who should be sitting in the cab alongside the driver only Raymie Boland. Large as life, with a pearly-gate grin on his face. The trailer behind him was stacked with furniture and various household odds and ends. I saw a lamp stand, a plain rounded table, an old wooden radio. Raymie unrolled his window and grinned down at us. But he spoke only to me.

'I'm outta here fer good,' he shouted above the engine noise. 'I jus' thought I'd put yer mind at rest, like.'

'Come away, Paul. Don't even speak to him,' Cora urged.

'Where's your Mam and Dad and the rest of your family?' I asked, not heeding Cora and not believing him. I assumed he'd just thumbed a lift on a passing truck.

'They're goin' be car,' he told me.

I glanced at the driver, and he nodded back. 'I'm landed with this here comedian,' he said. It seemed to add up. Trust Raymie to stick where the action was.

'Ma an' the oul' fella couldn't bear the noise off'a the mine,' he elaborated. 'I'll be a Townie from now on. Some crack, innit? We had us a whale of a time here, though. Me an' yerself an' the lads. A great time...'

No mention of the apple raid, or of me being locked all night in Magpie's shed. Raymie had a short memory when it suited him, as Cora said later.

The driver grew impatient. He pulled faces. He wiped his brow. He twiddled his thumbs on the steering wheel. Finally he revved and revved, but he didn't pull away. Raymie's voice faded into the engine racket. His lips were moving still, but I couldn't read them now.

Fact is, I probably never could read Raymie, soundtrack or no. He looked almost wistful, somehow. He looked sincere, more reasonable than I had ever seen him, nattering hopelessly against the engine. Maybe it was only the moment that mattered, with Raymie, and nothing beyond.

Briefly the engine quieted, and I tried to find a word to say, but none would come. He reached to shake my hand, but my hand stayed firmly by my side. And Cora put a grip on it, just in case. Then he looked almost bewildered as the truck started to move away. I turned to Cora. She and I did a spontaneous jig around the middle of the road. He's gone! He's gone! He's gone!

I could pretend to you that afterwards I met Raymie

Boland. That I turned the tables on him good and proper, and made him suffer for all he had put me through. I could perhaps spin the story along so as to work just such a flourish on it. But it wouldn't be true. What I can honestly tell you is probably harder still to believe. I actually cried, later that evening, with unaccountable sadness, upstairs on the porch roof. And when I went to bed, I did dream once or twice of bashing Raymie something awful. But no, the deed was never done. Happily, I soon let those dreams of vengeance go.

10

The Banquet

IN EARLY SUMMER a great banquet was held, to celebrate the successful start-up of Darkfield Mine. Everyone was invited, and nearly everyone attended. Dad had just bought his first, almost-new car, which he drove to the plush hotel where the reception was being held. I persuaded him and Mam to allow me go with them. Getting there was an adventure in itself, since Dad hadn't yet mastered the knack of driving. The passenger side of the car scraped against every other hawthorn bush, making Mam wince and click her tongue.

We first drove through the begrimed and bumpy 'mine road' to collect Magpie. He painstakingly removed the elephantine gas mask, his fingers clumsy with its several straps, before telling us he'd received no invitation.

'When did that ever stop you?' Dad asked.

'I'm not a discourteous man,' Magpie answered.

I smiled, knowing that he would attend precisely because he hadn't been invited, and he smiled back. Besides, I could see that he had just shaved, and was wearing his best, slightly crumpled suit.

'I'm averse to that auto mode,' he told Dad, pointing at the car, after they had talked for a while. 'I'll make my own way to the hotel.' He drummed his hand playfully on the car-roof. 'Well wear, regardless.'

The hotel car park was nearly full, and in a reserved area the Mercs and Jaguars owned by the directors of Darkfield Mining Enterprises were on sleek display.

'Haven't they only four wheels, no more than my own?' Dad said, and I certainly wasn't prepared to argue with his logic. Our neighbours sat at the lamp-lit reception-room tables. Most greeted Mam as if she were a long-lost member of the family returned. A few scowled at Dad, not liking his opposition to the mine. I glimpsed Cora and her parents, already seated. She beckoned or waved, I'm not sure which, but there were too many tables between us to negotiate. We didn't get a chance to talk.

The Bigwig who owned the mine said many pleasant things that night about us natives of Darkfield. 'Hospitable' and 'hard-working' were among the words he enunciated. He couldn't have been more right. Just look how well he and his friends at the high table were doing out of us!

He joked and talked, and cheers rang around the reception room, and glasses were raised. It was a celebration, and each new bit of news he gave fed fuel to everybody's wish to enjoy the good times. The lucky strike! The bonanza! The winning power words.

Mam looked as if she regretted that we had bothered coming at all. She and perhaps twenty others, I reckoned, looking about at the tables and the faces. For a moment or two, I even wondered if we were all just being a shower of misery guts, opposing the mine.

But when I thought of the mess already made beyond the Callows, and of the orchard pupae about to emerge – which would never have a chance surrounded by minelands – I knew we were right to oppose. So I ate the grub, and, though it tasted good, I didn't let it soften my resolve.

'What that fellow needs,' Dad said, tilting his head at Bigwig, 'is a good dose of medicine from Magpie.'

'Or from the Wise Woman,' Mam put in.

'Why did ye come if ye are against?' a man sitting opposite to Dad exclaimed. 'Ye knew what ye were lettin' yerselves in for, didn't ye?'

'We're here because we want to know what's being planned for Darkfield,' Dad told him. 'It affects us. It's the only way we'll know, because those fellows up above don't agree to meet us on our own ground. We didn't expect all this... this... this triumphalism.'

The man made no response. Just picked up his dessert spoon and dug into the ornate bowl. I felt like cheering Dad for having conjured such a hefty word as triumphalism. It certainly intimidated the other fellow. But where was Magpie? Shouldn't he be here by now?

'There's a special gate,' Bigwig said, 'a special gate we've been given. It's a golden gate, you'll be pleased to know. Not San Francisco's,' – he paused for the polite laughter – 'but a truly magnificent gate nonetheless. Twenty feet high, ornate spears on top of it, burnished gold, with four great stone columns to support it. It's been shipped in at enormous expense, a special bequest, and we will erect that gate as a symbol of the new-found wealth and prosperity of Darkfield, and indeed of this great county of Galway!'

Cheers raised the rafters at that. I quietly sipped my lemonade. Dad wouldn't allow me to drink alcohol. And Magpie wasn't with us, so he couldn't overrule Dad. But then Mam would have overruled Magpie. To be honest, lemonade tasted a lot better than Magpie's porter, anyway!

Bigwig hadn't finished yet. 'A new sub-station is being built,' he said. 'It will provide power for Darkfield Mine. I can guarantee your kitchen lights won't be flickering any more, dear ladies, when we have that in place!'

There was a slight sniggering at Bigwig's weak joke, but Mam was white-faced. 'The gall of that man!' she said aloud. 'Does he not live in a kitchen, same as the rest of us?'

Some people gawped back at Mam. But Bigwig heard, or chose to hear, only the laughter, and it seemed to hearten him further.

'At full production,' he said, 'Darkfield will use more electric power than all of this beautiful county of yours put together! Darkfield will become the brightest jewel in the landscape of the west.'

Dad was becoming more and more agitated by the minute. He shifted his chair back from the table. He was about to rise, to confront Bigwig, but Mam restrained him.

'Look who's landed,' she said.

We turned, and there was Magpie, making his way stiffly forward, leaning on the chairs and tables, venturing until he had reached the elevated place where Bigwig presided and where Bigwig's companions sat.

Bigwig gazed down at the intruder.

'And who are you, good man?' he asked, looking slightly askance.

'I go under the name of Magpie, but that ain't no matter.'

'Magpie, eh? A quaint name, certainly.'

'An iridescent name,' Magpie asserted. He was talking about the way sunlight catches the plumage of that brazen black-and-white bird, showing up green and mauve and blue, besides.

'I'm here to talk,' he said. 'To register my croak.'

A local man, a supervisor at the mine, whispered in Bigwig's ear, then Bigwig smiled indulgently and said: 'That's the beauty of democracy. Everybody gets an opportunity to speak. The floor is all yours, good man.'

Magpie stood back a pace from the high table, and jizzed himself up with a shuffle of his arms.

'People of Darkfield,' he said directly out to us, 'I appeal to you tonight. Don't sell your birthright to these be-suited gentlemen.'

His arm swung wide, indicating Bigwig and the other big shots. 'Don't sell your land for their promises. Leave it intact. It belongs to your children, and your children's children. You only have it on loan. Mind it for all the people yet to be born.'

'You're too late by a mile,' a woman shouted up. 'We've already sold, and you should do the same, if you have any sense.'

'We can reverse everything,' Magpie cried. 'For the sake of the children...'

'You're a fine one to talk,' a burly man interrupted. 'With no seed or breed of your own to provide for. If we were depending on you, Darkfield would be hungry and empty, except for the oul' snipe and the churchyard.'

A burst of laughter greeted the man's words. I could see Bigwig and his friends, who had looked temporarily uncomfortable, now begin to relax.

Magpie tried to continue, but people were rising to their feet, flinging their several voices against him.

'Sit down, Magpie, you backward eejit!'

'You're worse than the cuckoo in the nest. At least the cuckoo lays an egg!'

'You're an embarrassment to the people of Darkfield!'

So they abused Magpie, ordering him to clear off and not

spoil the banquet. I thought of the meeting he had held, months before, in the local hall. The same vociferous abuse was falling once more on his poor head, and it seemed that no enlightenment had been achieved.

However, Dad and several other members of AMID started to argue back against the pro-mine crowd. I felt heartened and joined in the general shout. It wasn't a debate – it was closer to a fight. I glanced at Bigwig. He sat with his arms across his chest, looking serious-faced. He acted as if he were listening respectfully to Magpie.

But Magpie couldn't be heard any more, and neither could Dad or the other anti-mine people. We were overwhelmed by boos and jeers, and when these had reached a crescendo, Bigwig stood to the microphone, waving his hands. Silence soon descended.

'I fear you're outgunned, my man,' Bigwig said. 'Fair attempt, though. Do join us in a toast.'

His words merely served to give the floor back to his adversary.

'Your false generosity don't fool me,' Magpie said. 'I know where you been. Fresh from bleeding a copper mine in South America, and another in West Africa before that. I follow your movements. I read 'em for all who don't. And now you're here, expectin' another windfall.'

'I'm here to make *everyone* prosperous,' Bigwig said in curt tones.

'You'll make yourself prosperous, and ruin us,' the old man said. 'You're preying on these people's hopes.'

'And the Magpie without tuppence to rub together,' a woman scoffed, stirring fresh hilarity.

'If you have concerns about the effects of the mine,' Bigwig said, changing tack, 'we can meet and discuss them with you. Our company has a proud record in caring for the landscape.'

'Open-cast,' Magpie said. 'Ain't that your record?'

'Yes, open-cast,' Bigwig agreed. 'The ore deposits are close to the surface. They're very workable. We'll landscape afterwards. We'll put the topsoil back. We're working even now on new strains of grasses, trees. We'll replant all after us.'

Magpie clutched the smooth white linen tablecloth, and gave it a little tug. Crockery and cutlery shifted, wine glasses threatened to spill. Bigwig's friends stood up abruptly, just in case.

'Ruination, that's all you'll leave,' Magpie said quietly. 'That's all you've left, wherever you've ventured. You'll poison everything. Ain't that what lead does? You'll break the mould, the set of nature. It will never recover.'

Then, as if to illustrate, he whipped the tablecloth off, upending all the repast. Bone china shattered, forks and knives flew with a clatter, and in the shocked silence I could hear the glug of a wine bottle spreading a red stain on the crumpled linen.

My heart was in my mouth. He'd be arrested. He'd be thrown in jail for this. But Magpie merely wiped his hands on a clean corner of the tablecloth, and walked slowly, sad-eyed, down the reception-room aisle, and away through the exit.

Whatever mischief, more sheer joy than mischief, was in me then, I felt my hands beat together – harder, faster, in solitary applause. Others joined in, Mam and Dad among them. But the majority roused themselves again to shout us down with loud booing. A local politician stepped into the breach at the high table, where waiters fussed over Bigwig and his party.

'Well, ladies and gentlemen,' the politician said.

'There's always a begrudger, isn't there, to remind us of our good fortune. But you know Magpie, of old. There's no great harm in him. He's a bit touched, that's all. I must, however, most sincerely apologise...'

'Touched' was a code word for crazy. I felt for Magpie, though. I knew he had spoken the truth. In another time, another place, they might build a statue to the likes of him. But not in Darkfield. It was too soon, too close to the bone. He was the oddity, the outsider, the scapegoat.

We went to look for him. He was retrieving his bicycle from where it rested against the pebble-dash wall of the hotel. Blue neon light from the hotel disco flickered against the side of his face.

'I'll pedal,' he said.

'I won't hear of it,' Dad insisted. 'You're coming with us.'

Both of them bundled the bike into the boot of our car, then Magpie sat into the back seat with me.

No one spoke for a good distance. Dad was a bit jumpy on the gear-stick. He veered close to the verge of the road. There was a familiar scraping sound against the window on my side. It seemed to free Magpie into speech.

'Mind them bushes,' he said.

'You spoke well tonight,' Dad said in reply.

'I acted discourteously,' Magpie said, sounding crest-fallen.

Mam assured him that his actions were perfectly understandable. He had endured a lot, living so close to the mine. Besides, actions speak louder than words, and his actions were a wonderful demonstration of the harm caused by open-cast mining. Everyone could see that, she concluded.

Such talk helped assuage Magpie's spirit. He had

regained his grin, and his determination, by the time we dropped him home.

'Remember,' he said, when we were parting after Dad had finally managed to turn the car outside his gate. 'Remember them Callows touch you, too.'

'They do,' Dad said. 'I'll see that no harm comes to them Callows.'

It was around midnight by the time we arrived back at our own house. Mam and Dad looked at each other. Then he covered both Mam's hands and mine with his two big hands. He tended to become a bit maudlin sometimes.

'I could build up the farm,' he said, eyeing us fondly, 'if ye pull with me...'

They both talked late into the night, making plans, and I was allowed stay up to listen. They would modernise the farm. Buy a tractor, new-fangled mower, swathe-turner, plough. They had some money saved, and they would borrow the rest. There were grants and schemes that they could follow up. I negotiated on behalf of Jack, our pony. Tractor or no tractor, I knew that the heart of the farm would be missing if he were sold.

'Sold!' Dad exclaimed. 'How could we sell him? Wouldn't we be selling our luck if we did that? You don't part with a gift from a good friend, do you?'

When Dad got started, there was no end to his run of talk. Mam and I laughed, hearing him get on his high horse.

❦ ❦ ❦

Next evening after school, I travelled the Callows once again to compliment Magpie for standing up to Bigwig. Or maybe that was just an excuse. Maybe I sensed how vulnerable he had become, and wanted to check in case he needed anything. I wasn't in any particular hurry so I took Magpie's sidewise criss-cross route over the treacherous ground, and in due course arrived at his little cottage.

There was no sign of him. His house was empty, and stranger still, his fire was cold. Magpie had always kept a fire. Sometimes, especially in summer, the hot coals would be covered with ashes so he could rekindle them easily next morning. I remembered his special word for that. Smoor. But today, the ashes were stone-cold.

I felt a sudden clutch of fear. I shouted from the haggard. There was no din from the mine, only an eerie echo, answering me.

I went into the orchard. The small green apples were abundant but there was no sign of Magpie. Feeling increasingly panicky, I went to the shed and opened its door. Our four pupae hung in the twilight. At least they were safe.

Suddenly Riff-raff bounded out from a dark corner to greet me. It seemed he'd not been let out at all that day. I took him back to the house, found some leftovers in a saucepan, and fed him. I watched him use his paws and teeth to get the food in, but my mind was racing in other directions. I felt sure that Magpie must be in trouble.

I racked my brains, trying to think where Magpie could have gone. Eventually I guessed – the old well! I hurried down the worn path to the well, with Riff-raff scampering after me, and there, finally, I found Magpie.

He had fallen into the well, and was groaning quietly. His head and shoulders were below the well's opening, which was at ground level. He wore the infernal gas mask. I removed it, gently as I could. His body seemed to have buckled somehow and become wedged in the tunnel, and it was this that had saved him from falling all the way to the watermark.

He stared up at me, unable to speak. How green those eyes of Magpie's were! Oddly it was the first time I had noticed their haunting greenness. I tried to reassure him. 'Hold on, Magpie, I'll get you out!' But when I got hold of one of his arms and tugged, his body wouldn't budge. He was stuck fast.

My heart dithered in hurt and panic. I looked about for something to render help. There it was – the dunking rope, attached to his enamel bucket! I undid the knot. It seemed to take ages. I reached down into the well, and managed to run the rope under Magpie's oxters. Then I drew out both ends, braced my feet against either side of the well, and tugged.

No use. I tried again. Still no use. I couldn't budge him. Luckily, because the rope was far lengthier than Magpie needed for fetching water from even so deep a well, I was able to fasten both ends securely to the trunk of a nearby tree, just to ensure Magpie against slipping any farther.

I'd have to go and get help. I thought of the mine nearby, but in the same moment the heavy silence reminded me that the workers had been given a day off on account of Bigwig's celebration. With each wasted moment I was growing more frantic. I'd have to go all the way back home to summon Dad! It would take too long! Then an idea struck me.

Jack, the pony!

I ran to the Callows and there Jack stood, browsing quietly. He let me come up close, then pulled his head to one side and swayed off in a lazy half circle. Slowly I closed the space between us, but again he swayed away from me. This time he shook his head.

I felt my temper rise, but temper would only drive him to the farthest reaches of the Callows. I tried another approach, stooping to the ground as if to gather a fistful of oats, then cupping my hands and holding them towards him. I clicked and coaxed. He started to come slowly towards me. He reached out his long head for a sniff. Then I had clutched his mane and swung myself on board. He wasn't prepared to gallop, but I dug my heels in and he worked up to a trot.

When I got back to the well, Magpie had started groaning again, but more quietly, which frightened me. I quickly undid the rope-ends knotted about the tree, and tied them around Jack's neck. I stood alongside the pony and pulled his mane while clicking my tongue.

With one step away from the well, Jack hauled Magpie out. I helped him by half lifting the old man onto the ground where he lay, exhausted. His eyelids fluttered once and then he became deathly still. 'Magpie!' I shouted. 'Magpie!'

I knew not to move him unnecessarily in case any bones were broken, but his face and hands were bluish cold. I ran to his house and brought blankets and pillows, and made him comfortable as best I could. Then, assuring him – though he seemed unconscious – that I would bring help quickly, I once again clambered onto the pony's back and rode hell-for-leather home.

11

Goodbyes

AN AMBULANCE BROUGHT MAGPIE TO HOSPITAL. We followed in our car. We fretted and fussed, waiting for news. The hospital authorities sent us home. Each evening after school Mam, Dad and I would journey back to the hospital, but Magpie was too weak to see us. Dad still drove too close to the roadside. He still scraped the car against the bushes. But he kept going, regardless.

'It's only a thing,' he would say. 'And a thing can always be replaced.'

He was frantic with worry over his friend, and though Mam wanted to be cross with him for ruining the glossy flank of our almost new car, somehow she just couldn't manage it.

We ought to have phoned, perhaps, and saved ourselves the travel, but we needed to be close at hand in case Magpie asked for us. Besides, we found solace just by sitting and quietly reminiscing in the hospital waiting room. Finally, on the third day, we were permitted to see Magpie. The nurse gave us only a few minutes. 'He's very weak,' she explained.

Magpie tried to drag himself up in the bed, when he saw us. Coughing shook him. A faded pyjama shirt fringed his bones. He seemed to have shrunk. His fingers, damp now, not cold, wrapped mine. His green eyes burned. He said my name several times, with ever-increasing faintness. My old name.

'Pauly... Pauly...'

Dad looked at me and smiled. He remembered that name. The name I had once fought to be rid of. The dreaded y. And strange as it may seem, it was the most beloved name to me now. Coming from Magpie's mouth, it was a beloved name. A name I would treasure always, because of him. The way I would treasure those things of nature he had shown me – his crickets, his Callows, his orchard, and the strange pupae that hung from his shed rafters.

Dad talked to him of old times, replayed old card games, drew down pranks they'd played on people long since dead. I thought he wasn't listening, that he had drifted off to sleep, but again his eyes flapped open.

'Go on,' he breathed.

So Dad talked of a donkey-cart which he and Magpie had once taken apart, and reassembled inside old John Hobbins' kitchen! Then they had yoked the donkey to the cart. When old John came home, he could never puzzle how donkey and cart had managed to drive through the narrow door of his house, or how he could get them out again! The story was tedious, far as I was concerned, but it seemed to console Magpie and Dad.

They operated in a time when people made their own fun. There were few books or toys, and no television. Dad said, 'We still had more fun than you youngsters do nowadays.'

'I don't believe that,' I said, and Magpie winked at me.

'Ah,' he croaked, 'you might be right.'

'Dad, aren't you much the younger?' I asked.

'I'm only half Magpie's age!' Dad laughed.

'Then why did you two knock around together?' I wanted to know.

'Children can be any age, can't they?' Magpie interjected, raising himself up on his elbow. 'I thought yourself and me the proof of that!'

'Oh, we are,' I managed, embarrassed at my mistake.

Neither he nor Dad talked about Darkfield Mine. When Dad asked him how he had fallen into the well, he whispered, 'A weakness came on me. I over-balanced myself.'

Then he lapsed back in the bed, exhausted, and closed his eyes. His body jutted thinly. His hands clasped themselves in a kind of pagan prayerfulness. The nurse hovered. She bolstered his pillow, made him comfortable. Dad and I rose from our bedside chairs. It was time to go. Magpie's hands fluttered gently, his green eyes opened, robbing us of retreats.

'He has pneumonia,' the doctor told us. 'His age is against him, I'm afraid.'

Mam had a theory about pneumonia. If you could suffer it for nine days, you would wear it out. You would survive. Then I consulted the Wise Woman.

'There is a crisis time at four to five days, the medical people tell me,' she said. 'We can only live in hope.'

When five days had elapsed, I began to grow more confident, though we were no longer allowed to see Magpie. He was attached to a machine that helped his breathing, the nurse told Dad. I counted through days six, seven, and eight. I concentrated so hard on making the moments pass that my head ached. And then, on the morning of the ninth day, a phone call came to say that Magpie was dead.

❦ ❦ ❦

Something broke inside me the day Magpie died. I cried and cried, and Dad – heart-broken too – held me close, and Mam held both of us. Eventually I went up to my room and flung myself on the bed. There was a dreadful constriction in my throat. I coughed and cried, but couldn't clear it. I gazed at the bare ceiling, then turned on my side and looked at the wall. The poster of Captain Valour had begun to fade. Its bright colours were being drained, browned by the sunlight. Soon it would disintegrate, be taken down, discarded in favour of some new poster – of a pop star, a footballer, whatever.

My eye fixed on the dull shard of silver, my keepsake from Magpie, still glued to the wall. It hadn't reflected Will o' the Wisp at all. The mine lights were too powerful. Dad had proved to be right.

An idea struck me. I went over and broke the silver shard from the wall. A chunk of masonry came free also, but I didn't care. I put the silver in my pocket, returned to the bed and eventually slept.

On the day of the funeral, we gave a lift to the Wise Woman, her husband, and Cora. The sun shone gloriously, but I would have preferred rain. I had always associated rain with Magpie, and with the Callows. I felt that the least the weather gods could have done was to pour rain on a good man's funeral.

Not many people came to see Magpie being put in the ground. Friends of his from the anti-mine protest group were there, of course, as well as some local farmers who had argued and fought with him but who stood prayerfully now, their cloth caps pressed in their hands. Tommy Hodgkins, the shopkeeper, who was famous for attending funerals throughout our part of the county, stood sombrely regarding the open grave.

Father Burke conducted the funeral rites. 'Ashes to ashes, dust to dust,' he intoned. He was taken aback to see me approach the lowered coffin and drop in my shard of silver ore. It fell with a loud clunk on the coffin lid. The earth would be shovelled over it, and eventually would claim it back.

'Magpie travelled far in his long life,' Father Burke orated. 'He travelled by means of books and newspapers, chiefly. His other mode of transport was the humble push-bike. He loved to walk the Callows. Some would say he strayed, but his heart was big enough to encompass the world. He and I often held theological debates. But gentleness was his abiding gift, humour his companion always. "What brings you, priest?" he'd say, whenever I visited. "I know it ain't prayers!" But let us pray for him now.'

I thought it noble of Father Burke to celebrate Magpie, regardless of whether he was a pagan or a prophet.

Afterwards, a middle-aged man approached Dad and Mam and me, where we stood at the graveside. He introduced himself and shook hands with us. He was Magpie's cousin.

'I'm sorry for your trouble,' Dad said.

'Thank you,' he replied calmly. 'But the odd thing is, I didn't really know him at all. Just today in fact, after I had arrived here in Darkfield, somebody told me his nickname was Magpie. I'd not heard it before. You seem to have known him well, though. I feel as if I should be commiserating with you.'

'He was a friend,' Dad said, snuffling a little.

'It seems he had few enough friends,' the man said, looking about at the gathering, 'but obviously dear ones.'

'He wasn't popular – if that's what you mean,' Dad said. 'But he stood up for what he believed in.'

Mam placed her hand on Dad's arm. Magpie's cousin eyed the three of us intently.

'Yes,' he said, 'I expect he did.' Then he walked briskly away.

We were to learn, later, that he had inherited Magpie's farm. The little house, the stretch of Callows adjoining it, the wonderful orchard. And we sensed that he had no fondness for these things. He would sell them to Darkfield Mining Enterprises, after a decent interval...

❦ ❦ ❦

Cora and her parents returned home with us. I moped about the haggard, at a loss what to do next. Cora loyally stayed with me. The mine had started up again. It seemed louder than ever, after its brief silence. Four giant haystacks had survived the foddering season, I noticed. They would be kept in store until next winter. 'There'll be less hay to save,' I said, and just then the words seemed to have no meaning, but I continued talking anyway. 'Dad's buying a new tractor, you know.'

'That's good,' Cora said.

'New and immaculate,' I said. 'He's going to teach me to drive it.'

'Better again,' Cora responded, humouring me.

'To hell with the tractor!' I shouted angrily. 'I couldn't care less about it.'

Cora was sympathetic. She said my anger was only to be expected. I was in mourning for Magpie, after all. It irritated me that she should be such an expert in grief as well as everything else.

'When someone dies, your link with them doesn't end,' she advised.

'It does so!' I exclaimed. 'I'll never see Magpie again, will I?'

'You won't,' she conceded. 'But you'll think of him, and your feelings of loss will change, even become happy, somehow.'

'How would you know?' I asked bitterly, for it seemed that if I were to go along with her ideas, I'd be committing something close to treason against Magpie, just fresh in his grave.

'That's what happened to me when Grandmother died,' she said quietly. 'It's still happening...'

'I'll *always* miss Magpie,' I said, feeling as sorry for her now as for myself.

'Yes,' she agreed. 'And you'll always be learning from him. You know, thinking what he might do next, in a certain situation.'

I wandered off towards the Callows and soon found myself stooping among bulrushes. A spiderling had spun its spoke-wheel web in a gap between two stems. It waited in the hub, golden brown, with a white cross on its back.

Suddenly, a wasp nudged close. There was hunger in its buzz. It explored under leaflet and stem, and then, before my amazed eyes, it seemed to entangle itself deliberately in the web.

Bravely the baby spider attacked it, but the wasp's jaws opened, snatching the tiny creature and in the same moment tearing itself away from the flimsy web. I was shocked.

'The spider is meant to eat the wasp!' I shouted, over and over. I didn't stop to recognise that this would indeed be the way, come autumn, when the spiderlings that survived had grown. In my grief for Magpie, I simply decided that nature had turned itself upside-down, now he was dead.

I ran all the way home and blurted out this story to Mam, who was standing at the kitchen door. 'Ah child,' she said quietly. 'Everything must eat, even the wasp.'

So that was it. That was nature. Everything must eat.

The thought of Riff-raff suddenly struck me. I had neglected him throughout Magpie's illness. I had clean forgotten him! He must be starved by now!

Mam didn't know what was the matter, for I broke from her without another word, back towards the Callows. She sent Cora to retrieve me. That girl could pick her steps at speed, for soon she had caught up with me.

'Riff-raff!' I panted, 'I have to feed Riff-raff! That's the least I can do for Magpie!'

Cora agreed. Our hurry made us take little care how we went, but luckily the floods had greatly diminished. Our clothes were soon muck-spattered as we swished through the rushes. The lace of my left shoe came loose. Then the left foot sank to the knee in mud, and I lost the shoe pulling myself free. Shoe and sock were sucked down into the mire, but we kept running, and the din of machinery grew as we ran. We were gasping for breath by the time Magpie's gate came into view.

The door to the galvanise shed was slightly open. As we entered I remembered the butterfly pupae. I had neglected them, too. But apparently that was exactly what they had needed – privacy in which they could be reborn. For there, above our heads, four ragged cocoons hung shrivelled from the rafters.

Cora, who had edged slightly ahead of me through the dimness, shouted. An astonished shout. I glanced immediately towards the one small window, and was awe-struck.

Its four panes of glass held each a giant-sized butterfly. Four glorious butterflies – fluttering their wide, vivid wings. Red and azure-blue and deep gold among the black spars and startling eye-patterns. I thought of the stained glass windows in Darkfield Church – where we had attended the first part of Magpie's funeral service – luminous in the sunlight. The wings rested briefly. And then they started trembling.

We knelt next the shed window, full of reverence for the butterflies, barely trusting ourselves to breathe. I recalled Magpie's phrase and I told it to Cora. 'Fruit of the orchard.' What would he call them now, he being a man of word-pictures and all? I cried for him there, cried so secretly that Cora didn't notice. I cried that he had missed out on this last, beautiful wonder.

The gorgeous butterfly wings flapped shut, then open once again. The butterflies wanted out. I tried the window's rusted hasp. It wouldn't stir. But still I pressed, and Cora added her strength to mine, and gently the entire window-frame gave away from us. The noise from the mine grew louder, infiltrating the shed. The butterflies dallied a moment, as if to gather their wits about them.

Their large pretend-eyes were within a fingertip's reach, astoundingly beautiful. I held my two hands flat in front of me, with thumb alongside thumb. That's how big the wings were. Yes, really that huge, though people have tried to tell me since that my imagination made them so. Wonder can make things bigger than they really are, but looking back through the years, I'm certain that those butterflies – just like the pupae they emerged from – were extraordinary.

The clanging, crushing mills of the mine seemed to quicken. Cora pursed her lips, and breathed gently on the downy bodies. They took flight. We leaned after them, our hearts fluttering. Where they were going neither of us could say. Maybe to the Indian sub-continent, I told Cora, or to the teeming rainforests of Rondonia. And she replied that Magpie alone might know.

I had done my best. I had kept my promise. Now I could only hope that they would find a good place. And perhaps a person wise and gentle as Magpie would make room for them there.

I imagined I could hear his voice, hoarse, exultant: 'They need no more. Let them go.'

Cora watched with me as they grew smaller and smaller, dwindling into the blue, evening sky. 'Wherever they are going,' she said, 'they seem to know the way.'

A snub coldness touched my bare foot. I turned. It was Riff-raff, nosing me affectionately. He looked thin and bedraggled. A pang of remorse struck me. Not only had I forgotten him in the fret and grief over Magpie, but I was forgetting him again now. Guiltily I patted his foxy head. He tried to nip Cora, out of pure affection, but I restrained him.

Outside, we found the half-eaten pelt of a hare. Riff-raff had survived by coursing the Callows! We both felt better, knowing this. Of course, nothing would satisfy him now but to follow us home. And what else could we do only let him tag along? The hares of Darkfield Callows would thank us for it! And anyway, as Cora said later, didn't he belong with me?

12

Epilogue

JUST YESTERDAY I RETURNED TO DARKFIELD MINE. It's long since been worked out and abandoned. For ten years or so, its lights were the brightest sights to be seen hereabouts. But funnily enough, now that they're quenched, the stars have come back into their own. And, to my eye at least, the stars are more restful. Let them shine.

The golden gate still stands. It looks as out of place now as ever it did during my childhood. Before being gifted to Darkfield, it had formed the entrance to a firearms factory in Birmingham, long since closed down. Who will have it next?

I thought of Magpie again. He was right about the tailings pond. It's still there. But it's not so much a lake at this stage, more a glut of poisonous mulch. In wet weather it seeps through the walls that were intended to contain it, and in drought it flies as dust.

The Crusher and the Concentrator Mill remain. The roofs of both have been blown off by the wind. And the mining area round about, vast acres of it, is covered with stockpiles of grey slag. Magpie's house is nowhere to be found, and the orchard he tended with such care utterly blitzed. A few thin blades of grass remain. That's all.

I went into the Mill for a look around. It is so huge that I managed to get completely lost. I cranked the handle of an old toilet. It still flushed. A fern grew from the bowl of an adjacent toilet. Everywhere was littered with broken glass, and strewn about were books concerned with geology and mining.

And then I found myself back at the long-deserted foyer. I was surprised to see old plans for re-landscaping Darkfield Mine still on display. Tattered posters showed photos of green fields. Captions promised a new strain of grass – a grass developed specifically for mining areas. It never happened. The company simply changed its name and moved to a new area. However the people at the new place had heard of Darkfield's plight and wouldn't allow open-cast mining. Magpie's struggle had alerted them...

The foyer's once-plush carpets were sodden with rain. I lifted a corner of carpet, and a centipede scuttled away from me. Further, there were mushrooms breaking through a crack in the tiles. And at the place where Darkfield Mining Enterprises had kept its ledgers and accounts, birds were building their nests among the shelves.

Magpie was right about many things. But I'm glad he was wrong about the Callows. The Callows live! By which I mean, they shake, they jump, they pipe, they drum, they whistle, they wade – and they let you down if you're not careful! The corncrake doesn't haunt the summer night air here anymore, but there's still plenty to see.

Come down with me. Bring a good pair of wellingtons. I'll show you around.

OTHER BOOKS FROM THE O'BRIEN PRESS

DARK SECRET

Frank Murphy

Davy's mother is dead. Davy's father is so wrapped up in his own grief he can no longer care for his son. For Davy, his world has been turned upside-down, he feels lost and lonely. Then he is sent to live with his grandfather, Batt Quilty, a shepherd in a remote valley in Kerry. He is a difficult man to live with. But there is more to Batt than meets the eye: his life seems to be lived under the shadow of the past. How much should Davy believe of what he hears, and can he trust Batt when the word 'murder' whispers through the valley?

Paperback £4.99/€6.34/$7.95

BIKE HUNT

Hugh Galt

The hunt is on! Niall's new bike has been stolen. He's out hunting for it – and cool operator Katy is out hunting for Niall, using her father's ham radio. Kidnap victim Wasserman escapes from a gang of ruthless gunmen, and they're out hunting for him. A fast-moving tale of thieves and kidnappers.

Paperback £4.99/€6.34/$7.95

THE JOHNNY COFFIN DIARIES

John W Sexton

Twelve-year-old Johnny Coffin is a drummer in a band called The Dead Crocodiles, goes to school with the biggest collection of Murphys in the whole country, and has a mad girlfriend, Enya, who owns a man-eating pet. Could life be any more confused? In his diaries, Johnny chronicles his problems with acne, isosceles triangles and his teacher, Mr McCluskey, who is trying to destroy his mind with English literature.

Based on the RTÉ radio series The Ivory Tower

Paperback £5.47/€6.95/$7.95

FROM EOIN COLFER

BENNY AND OMAR

A hilarious book about a young hurling fanatic, Benny, who is forced to leave his beloved Wexford, home of all his heroes, and move with his family to Tunisia! How will he survive in a place like this? Then he teams up with Omar, and a madcap friendship between the two boys leads to trouble, crazy escapades, a unique way of communicating and heartbreaking challenges.

Paperback £5.47/€6.95/$7.95

BENNY AND BABE

Benny is visiting his grandfather in the country for the summer holidays and finds his position as a 'townie' makes him the object of much teasing by the natives. Babe is the village tomboy, given serious respect by all the local tough guys. She runs a thriving business, rescuing the lost lures and flies of visiting fishermen and selling them at a tidy profit. Babe just might consider Benny as her business partner. But things become very complicated, and dangerous, when Furty Howlin also wants a slice of the action.

Paperback £5.47/€6.95/$7.95

Send for our full-colour catalogue

ORDER FORM

Please send me the books as marked.

I enclose cheque/postal order for £ . . . . (+£1.00 P&P per title)

OR please charge my credit card ☐ Access/Mastercard ☐ Visa

Card Number _ _ _ _ _ _ _ _ _ _ _ _ _ _ _ _

Expiry Date _ _/_ _

Name. . . . . Tel . . . .

Address . . . .

. . . .

Please send orders to: THE O'BRIEN PRESS, 20 Victoria Road, Dublin 6.

Tel: +353 1 4923333; Fax: + 353 1 4922777; E-mail: books@obrien.ie

Website www.obrien.ie

Please note: prices are subject to change without notice